ANGELS OF CAIRO

Gary Raymond is a novelist, critic, editor and broadcaster. He is the author of two other novels, *The Golden Orphans* and *For Those Who Come After,* as well as a non-fiction book, *How Love Actually Ruined Christmas.* He has edited a wide range of fiction and non-fiction books, from short story anthologies to political memoir. As a critic he has been seen in the pages of *The Guardian* and *The Daily Telegraph* and heard on BBC Radio Four's *Front Row* and Radio 3's *Sunday Morning Show*. Since 2018, he has presented *The Review Show* for BBC Radio Wales, and since 2012 has been editor of *Wales Arts Review*.

ANGELS OF CAIRO

Gary Raymond

Parthian, Cardigan SA43 1ED
www.parthianbooks.com
© Gary Raymond 2021
ISBN print: 978-1-913640-28-6
ISBN ebook: 978-1-913640-29-3
Editor: Carly Holmes
Cover Design: Syncopated Pandemonium
Typeset by Elaine Sharples
Printed by 4Edge Limited
Published with the financial support of the Books Council of Wales
British Library Cataloguing in Publication Data
A cataloguing record for this book is available from the British Library.

The following all took place on January 24th 2019, when Donald J. Trump was in the White House and a global pandemic that could claim the lives of millions of people was still only a predicted reality in the minds of the world's leading virologists and climate scientists.

The wheels of the porter trolley skate along the poolside flagstones outside the window of the ground-floor hotel room with the rhythm of a rollercoaster lift chain, and with every *clip-clack clip-clack clip-clack* Cliff's heart tightens as if he's nearing the drop. His fingers dig into the leather of the armrests, his eyes widen and whiten. Even though the sound fades as the trolley passes, to Cliff it stops dead, and his heart skips a beat. What's next? The wind in his hair? The screaming of his fellow riders? This isn't him. Anxiety. Fear. He's known hate before, but not fear. You think you know it, until you do, then you realise you hadn't known it at all.

How long can fear can keep him in the room?

The chair is soft, but not too soft; the temperature is cool but not cold. Hotel air. Frigid and still. No noise but for the trolley wheels, and they're gone now. He has kept the curtains closed. His suitcase remains unopened on top of the counter, his carry-on flung onto the tightly wrapped bed, the widest bed he's ever seen. Wider than it is long. All seven dwarves could have slept in it, side by side. If Cliff had been sharing it with someone, which he won't be, he would not have known they were there. He sits with his hands on his knees. The chair is the perfect size, height, width, depth, for this rigid pose to be comfortable.

The silence. It surrounds him like milk.

Cliff thinks of the flight. It already feels like a memory of a film, *from* a film, a sequence of well-cut scenes. Get in late, get out early.

The cabin is half-empty. Night flight. The white noise of the engine. All that recycled air, the egg farts and onion burps. Bodies stretch along unpurchased seats, heads on those small white synthetic pillows that have the texture of paramedic compresses for roadside trauma that Cliff always used to say were designed to remind you that you don't have a real pillow. Memory torture, he called it. Out the window, beneath, in the blackness, sometimes cities appear like leaves fallen onto a lightbox, a silent reminder on a gigantic scale that one day Mother Nature wants all this back.

Lewis is in the seat in front, his face lit by his tablet. Cliff's eyes keep flicking over to him, just to make sure he hasn't moved. The fear then was just a fizz, a rumble. It was denied any more life than that. Just a metallic taste at the back of the throat, like the aroma of old developing fluid he's used a few times when experimenting with film for a dream sequence he'd wanted to shoot. His dog had drunk some and threw up pink sick onto the kitchen floor.

Cliff gets up – his legs are stiff, airport-tired – and he walks to the bathroom to take a piss, moving slowly, stiffly, across the buffered marble floor patterned like nougat. His phone pings. It comes out of the air like a bubble popping in heated liquid. Sammeh. *I trust you arrived safely*. It's true; the logistics of the journey had been flawless.

Cliff ruffles his hair.

He's been overreacting.

Whatever went wrong, it was not as bad as it felt at the time. It's just a blip, he mumbles to himself. It cannot be as bad as all that. You're just tired.

He looks at himself in the bathroom mirror, his skin sallow in the plastic light. You're Bob Clifford. Robert Clifford. Little Bobby Clifford. And you have work to do here.

He leans on the counter with heavy shoulders. He flicks on the shower, pulls off his T-shirt and kicks off his slacks. Lewis is no-one to be frightened of.

It has taken Cliff years to get his movie made; long hard years of stand-offs, compromises, tears, perspiration, and specks of blood. His mother had died during that time and his chest cavity had absorbed it like a bell jar. Marie said she worried about him. She said it often. A kiss, the type that showed her he was thankful she was his girlfriend. Partner. Life-partner. What were they calling themselves now? This glorious union. They called each other different things depending on who they were talking to. Girlfriend. Fiancée. But they didn't have a ring. Without the ring it's just another word. A level up, but still just semantics. Cliff felt she talked to him like a girlfriend would. It's your funeral. That sort of thing. Not the wifely tone warning him of his responsibilities to the sanctity of their union, to an institution. A kiss, the type that landed on his forehead and smelled of morning coffee. *I worry about you*. A good few seconds looking into her glistening green eyes, and then her phone would buzz and she'd lean back against the kitchen counter. But the film was good. Marie had admitted as much. And he knew it. He knew others knew it. People said they liked it and he recognised sincerity when it was offered to him. He spent enough time with bad actors to know when he was being played. And now he's in Cairo, invited to present for consideration for the festival prize. *Invited*. The bubble broached. All those wrong turns, those curious avenues. The invitation began: Dear Mr Robert Clifford. *Bobby* now only to Marie, and she could have that. Childhood friends still called him Cliff. But it would be good to know who was calling after him in the street. He had made the right choice going for *Robert* in the credits.

A few days after the invitation came the call from Preston asking Cliff to take Lewis with him to Cairo. Cliff had been introduced to Lewis at a party. Lewis was mid-twenties, didn't blink, the look of a man, as Cliff's dad would have put it, who was always waiting to be called upon. Cliff hadn't given him a second thought. At least didn't give him much thought beyond when others mentioned him. *Have you met Preston's nephew?* It was always said over drinks.

Lewis talked as if he was reciting something. Something half-remembered. That was Cliff's memory of him.

"Why do you want me to take your nephew to Cairo?"

What possible answer could there be?

But Cliff knew what the answer was going to be.

"He wants to get into the movie business. He likes those Japanese comics. Introduce him to some people. Look after him. He struggles. Babysit."

Preston spoke in cascading rhythms, rhythms that did a job of alluring, of convincing.

Although not to everyone.

What was it Marie said about him?

"He talks in diarrhiffic waterfalls."

Was that even a word?

5

Cliff wasn't happy from the off. He told Marie he wasn't happy.

"Babysit. He said that. Exactly that."

"Tell him no."

"I wish I could. I'm not out of the woods yet with this film."

The kiss to the forehead, the smell of coffee.

"At some point you have to cut this loose and ask yourself what kind of artist you want to be," Marie said.

There was never any question about Lewis going with him. That's what Preston got for his half-a-million-quid investment in the movie. Continual affirmatives.

Cliff and Lewis connect at Heathrow.

Lewis fixes Cliff with eyes that in another context may have suggested they needed rescuing from something. Lewis looks uncomfortable in a crowd. He has narrow shoulders, no waist; his hair falls scruffily forward, a shake of salt and pepper at the temples slightly throwing off his youth. Cliff is immediately reminded of meeting Lewis at that party. They'd shared a moment of silent awkwardness similar to this one, only that time Cliff was half-drunk and the DJ was playing Soulwax. Now, though, Cliff is sober, and the only music is airline staff giving instructions to people who can't work the automated check-in screens. It's a busy morning, but the throngs seem to be concentrated in funnels of queues. There is a great deal of unused space. Cliff has an eye for unused space that often kept him awake at night when he was making his film. He had, he admitted, become obsessed with trimming things, making everything leaner. It was how he got the thing made. He's still thinking this way. His mind has yet to switch off from the filmmaking process, and it's morphed from maker to promoter without so much as the raising of a glass of champagne. That happened, surely – *of course it did*. Champagne *was* raised. Marie invited some friends over, but they didn't know why they'd come – they thought perhaps she was going to announce she and Cliff were expecting a baby or something, and when she said Cliff had finished his film the anti-climax reverberated around the house like a sonic boom. Cliff didn't register it. He probably even smiled and accepted some congratulations. But even at that moment, as the thin flute of bubbles was lofted into the air, he was concerning himself with how all this work must not be for nothing. Promotion. Get it seen. The work is not over. Not over. Not over. He could see in Marie's eyes that she could see in his eyes

7

that he wasn't fully present. At some point she would wonder if he was having a breakdown. He'd decided a long time ago to wait until she brought it up before he'd worry about whether she was on to something or not.

Lewis is a few people ahead of Cliff in the queue. That's how they meet. Face to face at the bend of the conga.

"It's good to see you again," says Cliff, and he holds out his hand, but the queue shuffles on and Lewis, with an awkward half-smile, moves past the outstretched hand, looking at it as if it's a prize he's missing out on.

Cliff puts his hand back in his pocket like he's clasping an IOU.

The queue shuffles on further. They meet again five minutes or so later.

Lewis says nothing.

"We've met before," Cliff says. "I don't know if you remember?"

It seems strange he wouldn't remember. It seems strange he wouldn't have been reminded, even. Preston would have mentioned they'd met before, wouldn't he? But Lewis's eyes are giving nothing back. If anything, he looks slightly scared. "It was at a party. Gina Forbes's. Her exhibition launch. At the Tech. The afterparty. I think Rhona introduced us. Rhona Brooks."

Still scared-looking.

"You don't remember?" Cliff is beginning to doubt himself.

The queue shuffles and they are parted again.

How long ago was that exhibition? Eighteen months ago? Three rooms, one with a DJ, one with a bar, four pieces hanging in each room. Gina was a photographer. As far as Cliff could tell, the photographs were extreme close-ups of buttocks, suggestions of crevices, cellulite giving way to the perfect smoothness of sand dunes. The fact the exhibition was titled "Unseeing the Lectures of Literature" did nothing to enlighten him. It was a stormy night, and Lewis wore a long black trench coat, and his earring hoop glistened off the glitterball.

Rhona, who had introduced Lewis to Cliff, gave one of her short sharp hand-offs.

"This is Lewis. This is Bob Clifford. He made a documentary a couple of years ago. I saw it."

She slid away.

"I've made more than just one documentary," Cliff said. "More than just one film."

Those beady eyes. Lewis sipped at his plastic-stemmed wine cup like his mouth was drawn on.

Cliff went on for some time about his films before Lewis said anything at all.

The queue has them back facing each other.

"Rhona Brooks introduced us," Cliff says. "You told me about your band."

Lewis seems to be thinking, as if, finally, he's giving this some thought. "The photographs of breasts," he says. "Yes, I recall. They were quite amusing."

A quaint moment, given what is to come.

Lewis is at the front of the queue now, and he is ushered to the check-in desk. As he walks over to it, he looks back at Cliff with pliant eyes.

An awkward, harmless start.

After check-in, and Lewis has waited for Cliff in one of the unused spaces to the side, there is a shift. A shift in tone, in atmosphere, in attitude – it's not so easy to pinpoint what the shift is, but Cliff detects it. Nervousness. Is Lewis a nervous flyer? Cliff had flown with a few over the years, most of whom had dealt with it by self-medicating. Booze. Pills. Lewis looks unsure in his nervousness. So, Cliff decides to set his controls to avuncular. Cliff is the elder, by at least a decade – probably more – the man of experience. And now it's just the two of them, no other queue-attendees eavesdropping. A simple question. It seems innocuous. Did you get to the airport okay? Something like that.

Cliff catches himself in the moment, shower water proving only a superficial cleanse. He pushes soapsuds out of his eyes with his knuckles. How long has he been in there? What *happened* in Heathrow? And after that, at security? And in the Food Hall, getting lunch in the café? And at the gate, as they queued for boarding? The five-hour flight? Immigration? Baggage claim? In the car, the car sent to pick them up? At hotel check-in? In the elevator? At the doors to their adjacent rooms? Cliff was damaged. Physically.

The flood, the deluge, the barrage, the onslaught, the artillery fire of a sophisticated weapons system.

Lewis's voice had been unstoppable. It burned the landscape of Cliff's psyche like a slow-moving river of battery acid, stripping everything to its skeletal essence.

At first, Cliff was blindsided. He didn't realise what was happening. He'd been good enough, in avuncular mode, to allow Lewis the conversational space to express himself. Lewis was the nervous younger of the two, so if he wanted to talk – if he wanted to talk a lot – then Cliff would give him the stage. But even then, you might expect gaps, pauses, inhalations. It was extraordinary how Lewis kept going, how he sucked the air out of the ground between them. It was paranormal.

The shower water runs over Cliff's head, the glass blades of water protecting him, encasing him in his own thoughts. The bathroom is a warming amber womb. Cliff is coming back to life.

He remembers looking out from the mezzanine over the shops and food courts. Lewis had gone to try and withdraw some

Egyptian money from the ATM. He returns. Cliff watches him approach daintily. Lewis walks on his toes, as if a giant has him by the waist. His brow is furrowed.

"No luck?" says Cliff.

The shower water now sounds like rain, that harmonious rain, the cleansing rain. Cliff can't remember – can't summon up the memory, more like – of what happened next. But it was that moment, after the ATM, when Cliff began to realise Lewis would not stop.

The flight might have killed him had he and Lewis not had the space to sit apart. Lewis goes to the Manga on his tablet. He is focussed intensely on it. Cliff leans his head back in the seat and steadies his breathing. After a while – and this is denial in action – Cliff takes a book out of his carry-on and loses himself in it. But when the plane lands and they stand, stooping to alight, Lewis takes up where he had left off when the flight left the tarmac in London. He had paused. Five hours before. And now he restarted. Mid-sentence.

Cliff looks at himself in the bathroom mirror, towel around his waist, dripping, pale, and he thinks about the shelling of allied trenches in World War One. Later, he would think of Japanese prisoner-of-war camps.

There's another message from Sammeh.

The car will pick Cliff and Lewis up from the hotel after breakfast to take them to the festival site. Cliff messages back. *How long is the car journey?*

Cliff sinks back into the soft chair, in the towel and those small white hotel sandals. He feels better now. Half-human. What had Lewis been talking about all those hours? The voice. Clean and clear. It had public schoolboy intonations, the straight lines with nods at international colour. There were some inconsistent long vowels and what Cliff soon decided were intentionally obtuse mispronunciations of everyday words. *Byudiful* instead of Beautiful. Nelson Man*dela* a cousin to the man*dolin*. The Tok of a tik-tok for *Tok*yo. Lewis's speech became an atonal language that Cliff's brain, used to the dips and bends of the sophisticated conversationalists of his acquaintance group, could not, ultimately, comprehend. Shellshock. There was nothing to pick from the blown-out soil of his mind. There he is again, returning to the trenches.

Lewis has written a script. Eighty pages in ten days. Hardly slept. But he wanted it done in time for Cairo. He intends to pitch it. He's printed it off. He taps the bag on his shoulder with a delicate fingertip like it's a hot kettle. Cliff is then given ten minutes on the problem with Lewis's printer. Then the *history* of problems with his printer. Then problems with printers more generally. Lewis is not afraid of the cliché. Lewis hadn't had such problems when growing up in Germany. There are no printer problems in Germany. That topic exhausted, on to the plot of his script. Heavily influenced by Manga and H.P. Lovecraft, but essentially a coming-of-age story; Lewis doesn't trust the term *bildungsroman* and when Cliff says the word here, Lewis goes ten minutes on why it's inappropriate. A coming-of-age story of the daughter of a diamond mine owner in Guinea, Africa. He says Guinea, Africa, like Americans say Paris, Texas. The movie opens with the collapse of the mine and ends with tentacular sea monsters in the desert. Along the way is civil war, a tea party, and a telepathic orangutan named Professor Profondeurs.

Routine next.

Lewis walks Cliff through his writing routine, although Cliff isn't quite sure why. Lewis seems to go into some semi-trance when regaling. He glares at Cliff when he's speaking, unblinking, as if they are the only two persons in the world, of which only one of them is a sentient being capable of thought and movement. Whenever Cliff manages to break the stream and offer a few words, Lewis gently recoils, his eyes drop and he pinches the skin on the back of his hands until Cliff stops, one or two five-word sentences later, and Lewis recharges, his eyes lock, and the monologue continues. The routine, Lewis's routine, as if Cliff has asked, and as if Cliff is an onlooker, a fan, not someone who has written ten scripts, made three documentaries, won an award at an international festival in India, and now has directed a feature, *this* feature. It's why they're both going to Cairo. It's why Lewis is going to Cairo. When the waitress brings them coffee in the Heathrow Food Hall café, Cliff feels the urge to reach out and grab her hand, plead for his rescue. So, by the time the plane is taxiing for take-off, and Lewis is exploring his own relationship with caffeine in a winding free-form verbal essay on the subject, Cliff has surrendered.

Marie would not have approved.

So, Lewis doesn't observe the same societal norms as what you're used to. Maybe he can teach you a thing or two. You could do with new perspectives. Get involved. Experience other people's lives.

It's easy to imagine her comments. But she doesn't *get* it.

Lewis goes on.

Cliff is soon hoping for visions of Marie's admonishments to rescue him from bleaker things.

He thinks of standing alone in a blizzard.

He thinks of Father Karras's mother coming up out of the subway in *The Exorcist*.

He thinks of drowning. *Gurgle gurgle*.

He thinks of the blood coming from the elevator shaft in *The Shining*.

He thinks of mobile phones causing brain cancer.

Of 5G causing pandemics.

The frequency of Lewis's voice, unwavering, scalpel-like slicing off the top of Cliff's head with a hairline incision and pressing rusted nuts and bolts into his brain like it's putty.

Marie would have scowled.

Please scowl, Marie.

The fact is, she just doesn't understand. Nobody does, nobody would, nobody will. When this is over, Cliff will be like a soldier coming home from war, isolated from his loved ones by trauma.

With Marie's voice in his head, Cliff dresses, bravely, convinced Lewis was an apparition, the whole thing intensified by the peculiar, heightened dreaminess of travel. How would Shakespeare have explained it away? Bad fish? A stuck grape pip? It was stress, the fatigue, the expectation of Cliff having his movie not just seen, but judged. It must have got to him.

At breakfast, Lewis talks.

He talks about his food, about his breakfast habits at home, about his home, about his mornings and his thoughts on the idea of breakfast in general, and things he's read about the history of breakfasts. He shares a flat above a veterinary surgery. He talks about how he used to help out there, but they eventually had to let him go no hard feelings business was slow cutbacks, and now it's slightly awkward as he still sees them every day particularly when he's taking the bins out as they share a side alleyway described in detail but he tries to be philosophical about the patterns of human interacting and what those patterns say about us as people.

My God, thinks Cliff. His flatmate. His flatmate must be deaf. Or dead. Or a priest. Or all three: a deaf dead priest. Or more likely his flatmate is just a supersized bag of animal feed propped up in the corner of the room with a face drawn on it with a Sharpie, like a craft version of Norman Bates's mother.

All this, and they haven't even eaten yet.

There is a trans-continental buffet, typical of these grand five-star hotels. Cliff watches as Lewis passes the fried rice, the aubergines, the fruits, the *kofte* and falafel, and hovers around the baked beans and beef sausages. Cliff has put a tablespoon of each basin onto his plate. It is a muddled tapestry of awkward culinary companions. When on holiday with Marie, he used to pile his plate like this to make her laugh and roll her eyes, but he grew to like the mix. Lewis eyes up the plate. Cliff has piled it conspicuously high. He is treasuring this quiet time at the buffet. Lewis asks if falafel is a breakfast food, really?

20

"If it's here, it must be."

Lewis then gives up the most terrifying sentence yet.

"I'm a vegan."

Cliff feels his heart grow hard.

"So, you can eat falafel," Cliff says, pointing at it with his fork. "But not the beef sausages."

Mmmmmmmmmmmmmmmmm.

This noise Lewis makes is loud, as if he's trying to reach the cheap seats. It's high-pitched, like something from the BBC Radiophonic Workshop. He tilts his head. He takes the tongs, puts one falafel ball on his plate. Tilts his head again. Replaces the ball onto the buffet basin. He makes the noise again. Tilts his head. Puts the falafel back on his plate. Cliff moves away, moves on, and looks back to see Lewis finally put the ball of falafel back onto the buffet. Lewis also moves on, back to the baked beans, but Cliff sees him looking back over his shoulder to the falafel. There's every chance this drama has a few more Acts to play out before it concludes.

Cliff sees a chance for a quiet few minutes eating alone.

From the table he sees a waiter go up to Lewis. Looks like he wants to help, but Lewis goes rigid. Cliff wonders if he should intercede. But he stays seated, washes down a mouthful of falafel, beans, and scrambled egg with some black coffee. There is nodding between the waiter and Lewis. Lewis comes back to the table and puts his plate down. It has some beans, some green leaves, and some couscous. The two men look across at each other for a minute.

"Everything okay, Lewis?"

"The man is going to bring me an omelette," Lewis says.

The restaurant is quiet, a few people eating alone specked around. They've thankfully missed the rush. Cliff is unsure of the correct time. He looks at his watch and it is still on GMT. It's 7:42 back home. Marie will be leaning on the kitchen counter now, coffee in one hand and slice of toast and marmalade in the other, her eyes glazed but her mind on the *Today Programme*. Cliff imagines her in grey slacks and a black blouse, the sun breaking in through the slats of the kitchen blinds and making her blonde hair shine like a halo.

Lewis is saying that he tries to eat a balanced diet. And here it comes. Cliff feels his head grow heavy. The speech about veganism. It's going to cut deep, this one.

Cliff's eyes are drawn to four men, Arabic men, you can assume they're Egyptian, in matching blue and black tracksuits. They come into the restaurant and take a table just across the way. Football coaches, Cliff thinks. Soccer ball emblems on the breast pockets of their polo shirts gives them away. They know how to order, and how to combine the disparate offerings of the buffet. Coaches of a touring team, perhaps. A high-school team? Cliff wonders about asking if they have any room on the tour. When he was a kid, and he used to go and watch his dad's team play on the Saturday afternoons, there was one man in charge of the bucket and sponge, who would run on if someone got cropped. Cliff could do that for these guys. Like running away with the circus. No need to worry about language barrier. The bucket and sponge is a universal language.

Lewis is talking about the morality of eating insects.

The car comes.

Lewis, at breakfast, has been talking about the evolution of horror literature. This isn't a subject that would normally repel Cliff. He is something of a horror geek, or nerd, or whatever the fans are called nowadays. But Cliff is not part of any fraternity. He views his dedication to the horror genre as something pseudo-academic and most definitely mature, serious, intellectual. He could contribute to this conversation, he feels, and in interesting ways, but there seems no way in.

"I'm a big horror fan," Cliff says.

But Lewis barely registers the contribution. His lips purse for a second while Cliff delivers it, and then they unpurse in order to continue on their way.

Lewis is talking about his own evolution too, but this is not biography, it is more a swirling essay on the psychological rift met within him by the impetus of the deranged authors of madness. He touches on Lovecraft again. If this was a documentary, and Cliff was interviewing Lewis, he would ask him what the *Ancients* represent to him. But this isn't a documentary, and Cliff isn't interviewing Lewis. This is breakfast.

And it continues as they walk out to the lobby. As Cliff walks over to the reception to ask whether their car has arrived, Lewis keeps talking. He must – *must* – reach the end of his story, his analysis, his evaluation. Even if it goes on forever. Into the shadows of time.

Lewis is silent while Cliff addresses the concierge, who walks the two of them out to the front of the hotel and waves at their car, which chugs into action and comes slowly before them.

The driver gets out. An older man, his English is good, not just functioning; it is fluid and he has a sense of humour. As he opens the doors, he says something Cliff doesn't quite catch, but there's something to his tone that makes him realise it was meant in jest. Cliff laughs. Lewis says, "What did he say?"

He says it loudly, as if the driver isn't stood right there.

Cliff looks at Lewis. The driver looks at Cliff.

Move past it. Move past it with force and confidence. That's the best way to deal with these stutters.

"How long does it take to get to the festival site?" Cliff asks the driver, as if Lewis has said nothing at all.

"Only fifteen minutes," says the driver. "But we have one pick-up on the way. A very slight detour."

The car is beautifully air conditioned, and the black leather seats are cool on the forearms and the back of the neck. Lewis continues to talk.

Cliff has time in the car to ruminate in a new fourth dimension of his mind, an anteroom to the reality around him. Wasn't Preston's brother, Lewis's father, in the armed forces? An officer. Brigadier General or something? Army life explains the German part of his backstory. Also, the rank, if remembered rightly, does suggest public school. A boarder, even? Cliff looks Lewis over. Perhaps it's a cliché, but he must have been a disappointment to a Brigadier. The earrings. The lack of blinking. The pinching of the backs of his hands. And living in a flat above a vet's? A suggestion he's estranged.

And this is where the Fourth Dimension merges with the strange world of the first.

Lewis is talking about his relationship with his father. Two roads meet.

Lewis was a disappointment to his military dad. His heroes were not Churchill, or Monty, or Horatio Nelson, but Eno, Schneider, and Czukay. Lewis wanted to form an electronica band, not go to Sandhurst. Cliff wonders if the Brigadier was relieved to be disappointed, to not have to send his son to that rarefied place. Lewis suggests he suspects his father had an original creative impulse when he was young that had been crushed by the necessities of the military mind. Lewis says he believes creativity is hereditary, and although he also believes nurture can be important, and the impulse could even skip a generation, it's still likely his dad suppressed poetry for prosody. He speaks about all this as if it's the plot of a daytime soap he's been watching and not his own somewhat sad backstory. Lewis goes on and on, and Cliff tries to take in some of the sights of Egypt out of the window of the car, the sand, the construction work, the grand sandstone homes of the suburbs with their shaded balconies and high-gated drives, the dunes of the horizon. And then Lewis says, "I think my father has always been a little bit afraid of me."

Cliff holds this for a second. It's sadness he feels.

Then somehow without drawing breath, they are back with Lovecraft and Innsmouth and cosmic horror, and how Lovecraft was probably an anti-Semite because he was mollycoddled by his mother and incubated resentment toward her for his perception of his own undermined masculinity and he was almost certainly a homosexual and self-loathing because of it and all this manifested itself as open bigotry.

Cliff senses a door opening in Lewis's mind.

An unfathomable realm where unending verbal essays on the horrors of the historical abuses of the tribes of Abraham awaits. A trapdoor, beneath which lurks an ancient many-tentacled creature. His ability to follow strands in the darkness, and to pull his victim down with him. Cliff can feel a tentacle wrap around his ankle.

The pick-up, the detour, is in the person of a small Italian woman, in her fifties with a swish of short silver hair and a worker's tan. She is dressed for hiking, in strong footgear, a scarf – a *shemagh* – wrapped around her neck and shoulders. She energetically spins herself into the front passenger seat and her rucksack lands in her lap. She wears a warm smile and leans back over the handbrake to shake the hands of her travel companions. She is Professor Francesca Mantonioni, and she seems genuinely enthusiastic to meet Cliff and Lewis. But before anything else, a quick conversation with the driver, in Arabic. She seems to be suggesting he takes a different route to the one he had in mind, but in the end she concedes, but she concedes as if she'd won the argument anyway and it just isn't worth the hassle.

"So, what brings you two to Cairo?" she asks, twisting at the waist to speak to Cliff and Lewis.

Cliff looks at Lewis, who has been quiet ever since Francesca got into the car.

"I have a film in competition here," Cliff says.

Francesca beams.

"That is wonderful," she says. "A documentary? I cannot wait to see it. What is it called?"

"No, it's a feature film," says Cliff.

Francesca slaps her forehead.

"Oh no," she says. "Forgive me. I am on the judging panel for the documentary prize, and I am so excited to be here, and to be asked to do this. Documentary filmmaking is a real passion of mine."

"You make films?" says Cliff.

"No. Well, not as a filmmaker. I have made many films in front of the camera."

"You act?" says Cliff.

Francesca frowns, but not with upset, more with confusion. Perhaps something is being lost in translation?

"Haha, no, I do not act." She gestures at herself as if to suggest she lacks the glamour necessary for that particular trade. "I am a Professor of Arabic, specifically Arabic literature in Egypt of the mid-to-late medieval period."

She hands Cliff a business card. Università Guido Carla. Rome. He's never heard of it. Is that more impressive or less? Maybe it's one of those places hidden deep in the vaults of the Vatican.

"But my second passion, my hobby, if you like, is documentary filmmaking," she goes on as she tucks her remaining business cards back into her bag. "Arabic in particular. I have written several books on the subject. Hence, being invited to judge this prize. I am so excited. Did I tell you how excited I am?"

"I didn't know there was a separate prize here for documentaries," Cliff says.

"Oh yes, indeed. It's one of the most prestigious in the field. But tell me about your film. I'm afraid I won't get a chance to see it here because of my schedule – it is so crazy the number of films I am scheduled to watch – but maybe I can catch yours on general release."

Cliff looks her in the eyes. What can he say? He has the pitch all memorised. Or he did.

Where is it now?

There.

The words visualised on a stone tablet.

Speak them.

Nothing.

Instead, shakily…

"I used to make documentaries," Cliff says.

Francesca lights up even more than she already was.

"Ah, wonderful! Any I have seen?"

Cliff always scoffs at this question – how would he know what you've seen? – but not this time. His cynicism is snuffed out by a feeling of excitement. What if she *has* seen one of his films? This Italian professor who writes books about documentaries in her spare time.

"I made one called *Timon of Calcutta*," Cliff says.

Francesca rises in her seat.

"My god, yes, I have seen that," she shouts, and Cliff finds himself up in his chair too and beaming. "You burned the theatre down," she says.

Cliff feels himself deflate.

That *is* the right film. But it's not the right edit. He cut that scene out eventually. This does mean Francesca has seen it streamed on the M-Flex site, who took pride in showing it as part of their Burning Buildings season. They used the early edit included as an extra on the Blu-ray release without Cliff's permission.

"You saw that version?" he says.

Francesca laughs.

"Yes, I did." And she wants to say something else, but something is stopping her, maybe her English, though it seems to Cliff she is searching unsuccessfully for the phrase *fucking catastrophe*.

"And that actor, the one who wanted to be Timon," Francesca goes on. "When he throws the plates of food over the wall, gifted to him by the owners of the theatre, just as they drive past…"

She is laughing heartily now.

"He was quite the character," she says.

Cliff agrees through gritted teeth and sinks back in his chair. He doesn't need those memories brought up.

"So, you are here with your first feature?" Francesca says.

"Yes."

"That is brave. And it is a victory. Whether you win or not."

She turns to Lewis, who now looks braced for something.

"And you? You are involved in this film?" she says to him.

Lewis almost flinches. Cliff wonders if he was even listening just now to his exchange with the professor.

"I am actually here to pitch my script idea," Lewis says.

Cliff waits for the deluge, the outpouring of twisting waterways as he explains his script, his process, his living arrangements, and his childhood anxieties all in one stream of consciousness. Cliff waits. He waits.

"We're here," says the driver.

The car pulls up to the festival site, a vast modern conference complex on the outskirts of the city, shaped like a mile-long shoebox complete with lid on. As Francesca leaps out the passenger side, she offers words of encouragement to Lewis, tells him he has come to the right place, that this is a great festival for networking and that for a western filmmaker it is a valuable gateway to another world of creativity. As she says this, Cliff is straightening himself up on the curbside. It feels like the drive took longer than his watch suggests. He looks up to the clear blue sky. It's a warm morning, a safe, welcoming warmth, and there is a breeze coming from somewhere. Cliff thinks, if there is a way to describe this weather it is perfection. How bad can anything be when you're standing here in this perfect temperature with the perfect breeze and the perfect blue sky.

Francesca is handing Lewis her card.

"I don't have one to give you," he says.

"Don't worry about it," Francesca laughs. "I am old-fashioned. But email me. Send me your script. I would *love* to read it." She turns to Cliff. "And sorry I won't get to see your film. Email me the title and I'll keep an eye out for it."

She hikes her rucksack up onto her shoulders, turns, says something in Arabic to the driver – look after these two, perhaps? – and she disappears with a bound into the throng of festival-goers congregating near the entrance to the site.

As he watches her go, Cliff locks eyes with a man he takes at once to be Sammeh.

"Sammy; everyone calls me Sammy."

Cliff has researched Sammy on Facebook and notes his profile picture is remarkably accurate, which is rarely how it turns out. Sammy has an intelligent smile, and he's a big man, rounded at the shoulders. He stands side-on to them as he talks, as if every sentence is an introduction to a guided tour of an exotic palace. Welcome to the festival, welcome to Cairo, welcome to all these movie lovers. And he gestures widely at the thickening crowds. Sammy has a round face, thick lips, grey flecks in a close-cropped beard, and a handsome twinkle in his eye. His smile, which is the slightest of things, connects to that twinkle like it's linked by fibre optic broadband. His voice is deep, not quite booming, but his consonants hit the floor like a bouncing bomb. The *big man* element of his presence is almost certainly from a glutinous love of life – food, wine, the usual stuff. Cliff recognises that gregarious stance – it's something you can't imitate.

Lewis says his first words: "I have a script." Cliff wonders where that came from. Sammy laughs, slaps Lewis gently on the shoulder, and says, "Then you will love it here."

He walks his guests through the gates, armed guards wave them through. For a big man, Sammy moves fast, and Lewis and Cliff skip a few steps to keep up with him. They move across lawns and across walkways toward the entrance to the conference centre. Crowds part like it's a choreographed scene from a movie.

"We are so excited to have you here, Robert," Sammy says.

Cliff is looking at Lewis; calm, quiet Lewis, who hasn't said a word since he mentioned his script.

"I am very excited to be here," Cliff says. "I can't thank you enough for the invitation."

Sammy nods and grins.

"I am looking forward to seeing your movie," he says.

They move into the Main Hall through large glass revolving doors and step into an enormous mall-like auditorium.

"You haven't seen it?" Cliff is surprised. Perhaps he has misunderstood. But Sammy confirms.

"No." He puts the palm of his hand across his heart. "I am not on the selection panel. My daughter, Rana, she saw it in London. Preston gave her a private screening. She speaks very highly of it."

Cliff hasn't heard this story before. Preston hadn't mentioned it. Cliff's heart holds steady.

"When will it be shown?" Cliff asks.

Sammy booms, "Tonight!" And then he says, "You got my email? Preston forwarded you my email? With all the details?"

They walk fast through the auditorium, through crowds. Sammy is checking Lewis is still with them. Calm, quiet Lewis.

"No, no, I didn't get any email from Preston. Not forwarded from you."

Sammy laughs that big laugh of his and he throws his hands in the air and stops walking, turns to Lewis and he says, "That fucking uncle of yours. He is useless, no?"

They both laugh and Cliff watches them.

"You don't have to tell *me*," Lewis says, and he cocks an eyebrow.

And nothing else.

He stops right there and says no more.

They walk on.

Cliff realises he might need to know what was in the email.

Sammy says, "You brought the movie, right?"

Cliff is almost at a canter.

"What?" he says.

"You brought the movie," Sammy repeats.

"What do you mean *brought the movie*?"

"So we can show it to the judges."

"You don't have a copy?" Cliff says.

He says it, sure that's *not* what Sammy means.

"If I had a copy, I would have seen it by now."

And then Sammy stops, recognising a problem, looks at Cliff, looks at Lewis, Lewis shrugs with tight shoulders – has he even been listening? – Sammy looks back at Cliff.

"You come to a film festival to promote your movie," Sammy says, "without a copy of your movie?"

Cliff shuffles his weight from one foot to the other.

"I didn't know you didn't have a copy," he says.

"Preston said you'd bring it," Sammy says.

"First I'm hearing of it." There is an awkward silence between them all. "How much of a problem is this?"

Sammy looks thoughtful; perturbed but thoughtful. The crowds seem to fall away around them. He scratches at the grey patch in his beard. Cliff wonders if the discolouring is a result of this common usage, a contemplative scratch patch.

"He's fucking useless, your uncle," Sammy says, his grin now more serious, more annoyed.

"You don't have to tell *me*," says Lewis.

Cliff squints at Lewis.

They walk on at speed through the crowds toward the escalators.

"Don't worry," Sammy says. "We will get it sent over via the internet."

Via the internet is a strange expression, although Cliff cannot quite put his finger on why that is. Is it because it's archaic? Or because it sounded vague, unsure, a bit of a punt?

Perhaps it's a tactic to deflect stress, but Sammy changes the subject.

"You two are friends?" he says over his shoulder.

"Sure," Lewis says.

And he leaves it at that.

He does not elaborate.

Cliff eyes Lewis suspiciously, he hopes not too obviously.

"We don't really know each other very well," Cliff says, immediately regretting the eagerness with which he felt it come out.

"So, you have been brought together for this trip?"

"Yes," says Cliff.

Sammy gives that big grin of his.

"The start of a beautiful friendship," he says. "You know the movie?"

Lewis looks blank.

"You know the movie? The start of a beautiful friendship?"

"Yes yes," says Cliff. "*Casablanca*. Who doesn't know that movie?"

Sammy chuckles, to himself mainly. "The start of a beautiful friendship."

Cliff had always been mesmerised by the lighting of that scene, how the suggestion of mist is also the suggestion of the world beyond the airfield, the one Rick Blaine and Louis Renault have to go back to, the world that dominates the film and damns its characters. He'd thought about shooting his movie in black and white, but without using filmstock monochrome only looks parodical, and he couldn't ever have afforded real actual hold-it-in-your-hand film. Plus he raised it with Preston once, shooting in black and white, during one of their flirtatious lunches where Cliff was still trying to get some money out of him, and Preston just lifted a piece of whitebait to his lips on the end of a stainless steel fork and before popping it between his peg-like teeth he said, "No. Colour or I walk. And you can pay for the fucking lunch."

As the three of them rise on the escalator to the mezzanine, Cliff looks out over the vast conference hall, thousands of stalls and displays, producers, studios, freelancers, agents, from all over the world, stretching on as far as the eye can see. For a second, he thinks he can see the top of Professor Francesca's silver head bounding through the crowds, but he loses it quickly and cannot find her again.

"The documentary prize is very prestigious, I hear," Cliff says, tapping his fingers on the rail, trying to distract himself from any impending difficulties with his film.

"Oh yes, very," says Sammy. "But I don't have too much to do with that side. It takes place in the hall next to this one. It is twice the size. Four thousand stalls."

Sammy is a co-founder of the festival, but he doesn't run it, he isn't the director; he sold it on, and now he runs the prizes and sells his own movie ideas as a writer and buys those of others as a producer. Somewhere online, Cliff read Sammy is involved in around sixty movies a year. Cliff passes this over in his mind as they reach the mezzanine. It's impressive, he thinks; all this.

Sammy's office is a hub, several rows of desks peopled by his team, all looking up from computers to get a look at the guests. Sammy introduces each one individually, most of the names evaporating before Cliff can get a grip on them in his mind. Smiling faces, men and women, young, bright eyes and soft pleasant handshakes. The last to be introduced, a young woman who comes from the back of the room, is Rana, Sammy's daughter, procurer of Cliff's movie and the person who seemingly pulled the short straw and had to sit with Preston to watch it. She is tall, has a perfect complexion, made all the more luxuriant by her large dark eyes; she wears a headscarf, as all the women in the office do, and it seems to frame an inquisitive, thoughtful face. She says to Cliff that she enjoyed his film very much, and Cliff attempts a look of modesty and says, "I'm sorry you had to watch my film on a small screen."

Rana gently shrugs and looks at her father. Cliff is unsure whether she really understood what he was saying. As if some guidance comes from Sammy's blank face, she looks back at Cliff and smiles and nods.

"Your mother," she says, "in your film; she is very beautiful."

"Not my *real* mother," Cliff says with what he hopes is a charming smile. He has decided to push through the language barrier and keep at it. "Unfortunately," he says, widening his smile. He notices he is ever-so-slightly bouncing on the balls of his toes.

Nerves.

Why did he say *unfortunately*?

He is frowning. At himself.

He meant both that his mother was not as glamorous as the actress he found to play the mother-character in his film, but also that his mother is no longer around. But it sounded as if he was bemoaning the looks of his real mother.

Sammy steps in and says his daughter has great cinematic taste but her English is a little shaky.

Cliff catches this.

"Her English? So how did you understand my film?"

"She understands perfectly," Sammy says nodding earnestly, as if the weight of delivery should be enough to assure Cliff of something. He puts the tips of his fingers to his mouth. "Her speech is what is shaky. Her expression. She understands perfectly."

He then speaks in Arabic to Rana before turning back to Cliff and explaining, "I asked her to get in touch with Preston and have the movie emailed over to us as a digital file." He then puts his hand on Cliff's elbow and ushers him and Lewis over to a pair of upholstered chairs against the wall in the corner of the office, and offers them both tea.

The moment Sammy is gone, Lewis begins to speak.

Lewis *speaks* first about his scepticism that a digital file big enough to house a feature film would make it through by this evening, particularly if the Wi-Fi in the hotel is indicative of Egyptian coverage in general, and anyway the quality would probably be SD and be quite unsatisfactory for a director with any self-respect entering for an international prize and wanting it to look as crisp and clean as it was intended, or indeed as grainy and celluloid as was intended depending on the vision of the director, as Lewis goes on to explain that he understands the attraction of film stock, of the textures it gives an image and perhaps even as it places the auteur in a filmic tradition and brings to mind the great work of great directors, and who doesn't want to be sitting at the top table, nothing wrong with pulling out as many stops as possible to give that impression, and he goes on to say he would consider shooting at least some of *his* film in black and white and that the only way to do that properly would be to use film and that his movie will – not *would*, but *will* – be shot with a mix of film and digital, particularly because that won't be jarring given there will be animation, drawn and stop motion, plus top-of-the-range CGI, especially as Lewis intends to upend the old maxim of only showing the monster in the final Act.

Cliff stares at his companion, his eyes narrowing.

Lewis goes next to the allure of digital formats. Perhaps it makes him "uncool" – air quotes his; his fingers seem to creak like an old leather wallet as he bends and releases them twice. Is it "uncool" to be such a fan of the crisp and clean digital image in this day and age of hipster nostalgia? Lewis believes that eras have a look, a feel, and we have a duty to present our own eras in our own ways and not capsize progress for the sake of our own inward-looking titillation.

Cliff doesn't honestly understand everything Lewis is saying, but some of that is down to his own mind batting away words, cutting holes in the sheet metal of noise. Now anecdotes about a computer science class Lewis once took when he'd left "the family home" and was fending for himself, and how he was impressed with the teacher, a young Chinese lady – no air quotes this time, but it probably could have done with some – and then on to how China will perhaps be the only Super Power one day but first global warming is likely to have a say in it seeing as much of China's tech industry is built on floodplains. Interesting.

Sammy returns with two black teas in paper cups too hot to hold. Lewis sits there quietly sipping from his, moving the cup gingerly from one hand to the other and then back again.

Cliff rolls his shoulders.

"How is Rana going to get hold of Preston for the film if her spoken English is not good?" says Cliff.

"How will she contact Preston? Telephone," Sammy says, and he smiles. He then turns to Lewis and pulls up a chair. "So," Sammy says, "Tell me about your script."

Cliff's heart sinks.

But, my film.

Lewis seems to have become rigid, his back is straight, his neck locked, his thin lips patting at each other. Lewis looks at no-one.

Then he goes.

Strap yourself in for a ride.

"It's the story of a young girl who doesn't get on with her father, and she pretends that she does. And it has a supernatural element."

And then there is silence.

That is all Lewis says.

Sammy is nodding thoughtfully, and he curls his bottom lip.

"I like it," he says, and slaps his knee and begins to laugh. "Like my Rana and me," he says. He laughs louder. Eyes are peering over the tops of computer monitors. "She loves me, y'know," Sammy says; "But also, I know I am, how is it you say, a massive pain in her arse. But she's noble enough to pretend I am not. So, I like your script idea. It is very relatable. And who doesn't like a supernatural element?"

Sammy laughs and Lewis joins him as if trying out laughter for the first time. Cliff watches them both through narrowed eyes. Lewis asks if he can use the washroom and Sammy points him across the mezzanine.

When Lewis is gone, Sammy turns to Cliff and says, "Is he okay? He doesn't seem to talk much?"

Cliff feels a twitch come to his eye.

Lewis is gone a while.

Cliff and Sammy have been discussing Cliff's film, how he pulled it together, how he pulled it off. Sammy is particularly interested in the mechanics of production, of finance in the UK, of all that energy needed just to make a bell ring. His words. He talks with passion. He leans forward and shakes his fist, purses his fingers and shakes his wrist. He slaps Cliff on the knee.

"Tell me more about the money. Is it easy? Is it hard? Who do you go to? Is everybody like Preston Proudfoot? What does the landscape look like? Money. Money. The Milk of Human Kindness. How did we ever tell stories before *Money*?"

He opens his chest and laughs loudly, each time bringing the office to a standstill for a second, as if an expected tremor has shaken the building. Cliff is wondering if Sammy is thinking of branching outside of Arab cinema. Sammy leans forward, his elbows on his knees, his plastic chair too small under him. Cliff has not touched his tea. Sammy eyes it. Cliff eyes him eying it. He takes a long gulp of it.

"I will check on Lewis," Sammy says, but Cliff stands with him and they both go out of the office onto the mezzanine, Cliff glancing anxiously over to Rana as he follows. She is on the phone, a blank look across her face, impossible to read.

The crowd has thinned, pockets of people, young men in jeans and T-shirts, young women dressed similarly but for the headscarves of some, rucksacks hoisted over both shoulders, kids really, hanging out, talking films. The mezzanine is lined with breakout rooms, booked for press conferences, launch receptions, panel discussions on countless subjects from the current role of the war movie in political discourse, to the legacy of the cinematic legacy of the Marvel Universe, to the cinematic legacy of the DC Universe. In the far corner, some young women form a queue to the door of the smallest room for a discussion on Agnès Varda. These rooms hover above the cattle market below, the vast hangar of stalls and kiosks. In comparison it is heavenly, serene, shaded from the throngs and tumults of the lanes of hungry networkers. The kids up here, they look like students mostly. Cliff is sure the demographic changes as the day goes on and the press loosen up and the networking spreads to the breakout rooms. But for now, it has the air of the naïve hunger of youth about it. Ideas. Passion. Remember those things?

Editing. Cliff thinks of the frozen girl in the opening scene of Agnès Varda's *Vagabond*. We will find out how she got there, in flashback, but not why. Never why. Life doesn't give us such neat little explanations. There is no smooth transition in the way Varda compiles her scenes. When he was young, a friend of Cliff's used to say, "Life is built of chapters, and once you realise that is the structure, leaving things behind doesn't feel so traumatic. Move from one chapter to the next. Like in a book." But this isn't true, is it? Cliff has one eye on his fortieth birthday, even though it's still a couple of years away. He hasn't got here through chapters. Life has been more like the elliptical editing of an Agnès Varda movie. At the end we'll see the frozen body of a young girl. And we won't know why she froze. And it will be the end and the beginning also. Cliff had forgotten about Agnès Varda. He should have edited his damned film with a little more intelligence. A little more honesty.

Across the mezzanine, Cliff and Sammy both see the pale stiff figure of Lewis. He's in conversation with an older balding bespectacled man in a shiny black leather jacket. Lewis is holding his script in his hand. Cliff hadn't even noticed Lewis had taken his bag with him. The script is open, unfurled from its elastic band, the pages curled at the edges, Lewis looking like a street preacher with a large print Bible. He is pointing at the pages, his small expressionless face jutting out into that of the leather jacket man.

What the fuck is Lewis doing, and who is he doing it to?

The man, his victim, is feigning interest. Cliff recognises the look. He's seen it plenty of times over the years, sometimes opposite his own impassioned speeches.

Sammy says, "Ah, let me introduce you to this man, a very dear old friend, a *Great Man*."

He marches Cliff across the mezzanine. The man calls out Sammy's name as they get closer and throws his arms in the air.

"Sammy, this is your guest from the UK? I am loving his crazy script idea."

He has a big smile, like an animated shark.

Sammy corrects the man.

"No, *this* is my guest, and this is Lewis, the guest of my guest, and representative of the producer of my guest's film."

Cliff doesn't like any of those descriptors.

"Robert, this is my old friend Mahmoud, and he just happens to be the finest film critic in all the Arab nations."

Both Egyptian men laugh loudly at this, but Mahmoud does not contradict his friend. Mahmoud leans in and shakes Cliff's hand. The body language of Mahmoud is warm, welcoming, enthusiastic, but his words remain focussed on Lewis's script.

"Magic and monsters but it also has real heart," he says. "Has he told you all about this, Sammy? You should think about buying it." Mahmoud looks Cliff in the eye. "Are you his agent?" he says.

"No, Mahmoud," Sammy says. "I just told you; he is the director of the UK entry for the debut prize."

Mahmoud looks for a second at both the British men with slight confusion. Cliff wants to correct Lewis's role in all this but does not want to call him a *representative of the producer*; after all, Cliff was one of the producers as well as the writer and director. Preston was just one of many financiers; but he also doesn't want to contradict or correct Sammy.

"Lewis is my travel companion," Cliff says, and it cuts through the hubbub and every single person in that entire auditorium – thousands upon thousands of them, some of them have climbed awnings to get a vantage – seems to stop and turn to look at him.

Mahmoud looks at Sammy and then at Lewis and then back at Cliff. Are they about to laugh?

Could Cliff have made it sound any weirder?

Travel companion.

"Like… erm…" Where is Sammy going with this? He has a cheeky smile on his face and puts his chin into his hand thoughtfully. "Like… erm… Joan Fontaine in *Rebecca*?"

Sammy chuckles at his own joke and Mahmoud joins in. These guys know their western cinema.

"So, you're a filmmaker?" Mahmoud says with great mercy. "Which one is yours?"

Cliff clears his throat and shuffles on the spot.

He says, "It's called *Last January*."

But he's left off the important indefinite article and he has to repeat it: "*The* Last January."

And he repeats it again as if doing so erases the first mistake and starts anew: "*The Last January*."

Mahmoud seems to be trying to locate this title in his memory banks, and eventually he says, as if to the air rather than to Cliff, "I don't like the title so much. Not very memorable."

"It speaks of the central theme of the movie," Cliff says or wants to say. "Finality. Beginnings. January. Looking both forwards and backwards."

Mahmoud goes on.

"But a title must be memorable," he says. "How do you say, Oh, darling, shall we go to the cinema this evening to see what's it called something to do with January or something? What's it about? January? Maybe it's about being depressed after New Year parties? I lived in England for a while. That is a thing, right? You all get very sad in January. No, no. Nobody wants to go and see a film about January, the title of which they can't remember in the first place. Maybe we just go and see *Iron Man*. You know? It is about a man in an iron suit. You need a good title."

Cliff stares at Mahmoud.

"Who talks that way about going to the cinema?" he says or thinks he says.

Nobody talks that way.

He looks to Sammy and then to Lewis for some back-up, but he gets neutrality.

"What has *Iron Man* got to do with anything?"

Mahmoud laughs and it develops into a mild coughing fit. Sammy begins to slap him across the back, and he casts Cliff a quick glance as if he were the cause of it.

"Relax," Sammy says. "Mahmoud is just pulling your leg."

Mahmoud rounds off his coughing and straightens himself up.

"When is your film showing?" he says. "I haven't seen the schedule yet. The judges are always the last to know." Mahmoud grabs Sammy by the shoulder and rocks him, laughing grizzled through his teeth.

"It is on tonight," Sammy says before Cliff can answer. "You have the schedule, old man. You just haven't taken it out of your pocket yet."

They're ribbing each other. Nice to see, but Cliff would like to get some things straight before the frivolity begins. Like if his film *can* be shown tonight.

"First showing?" Mahmoud says, and he rolls his bottom lip and nods his head approvingly. "Last never wins," he says. "Everyone is tired, full of food and late nights. Most judges snooze through the last film of the competition. It is a good sign."

Could do with some of those.

Mahmoud straightens, and Sammy leads him off a few yards away, excusing himself for a second. Cliff watches, slightly dazed, slightly bemused, as the two men chat closely in some kind of conspiratorial union.

Then he feels eyes on him.

Lewis.

Lewis is standing next to him with that blinkless gaze fixed on Cliff's head. It's coming. Cliff can feel it, like projectile vomit, it's coming.

And then it comes.

A recreation of Lewis's conversation with Mahmoud, only Lewis can't remember Mahmoud's name and he taps his forehead trying to recollect it. Lewis opts for *that critic man over there*, and then goes on to quote seemingly verbatim all the positive things that critic man over there said about his script. That critic man over there understands the visual dynamics of it. That critic man over there understands the emotional undercurrent. He wants to know more, wants to hear more, wants to understand the vision better because Lewis wants to direct this script himself and although he'd resisted the temptation up until now, the time he has spent in Cairo with these people has proved to him he has the vision to take the helm himself and now he will have to insist on it as being not only the right thing to do but to some extent there is a moral imperative to it, and of course he would direct… of course he would. OF COURSE.

OF COURSE.

OF COURSE.

OF COURSE.

And now Lewis is explaining the visual dimensions to Cliff, and how the sand will burn like mustard and will part like waves for the tentacular sea creatures, but he also wants the textures of pen and ink like one of his Manga artist heroes, the name of which Cliff can never really pick out whenever Lewis gets into his stream-of-consciousness monologue on the genre, and the texture will be rich and subtle and informed by a deep emotional understanding of Japanese culture and my god he's going on to talk about Japanese culture now and we seem to have left his script behind for a moment in favour of a cultural critique of Japan, and then to Lewis and how he cannot really pinpoint where his admiration for Japanese culture comes from, and he runs through a bullet-point list of the things he admires about Japanese culture and Cliff feels himself looking Lewis up and down, evaluating his physicality. Is he about to attack Lewis? It wouldn't take much to flip him over the balcony and off the mezzanine, tumbling to the crowds and concrete below. Not much at all.

"I should have said that Mahmoud is a judge for the feature film prize."

Sammy is back.

Cliff snaps out of it.

Rubs the back of his neck with the moist palm of his hand.

Lewis is still and silent.

"Is he?" Cliff says. "Not a good sign if he can't remember the name of my film."

Cliff laughs nervously.

Sammy imitates Cliff note for note.

"Don't worry," Sammy says. "He was pulling your leg about the title. *The Final January* is very memorable."

"The *Last* January," Cliff snaps. "*The Last January.*"

Sammy ushers Cliff and Lewis back to the office.

Rana is at the rear of the room on the phone. She is pacing, biting her bottom lip. Nodding.

Nodding is good, right?

Cliff has barely registered it, but Lewis is at his side talking into his ear saying something about a dog that died, that was put down, at the vets back in London where he used to work, the one he now lives above. Lewis hadn't been expecting the dog to die. To be put down. It was that moment in life where grim reality buffers with an intellectual and therefore emotionally disengaged understanding of the cycle of life. They froze the dog. They do this with all animals they have to put down, until they can do whatever it is that's right and proper. Frozen in a chest in the back room. The death of a dog, even a stranger's dog, is a primal attack on the heartstrings. Lewis explains how he had a borderline panic attack, something he hadn't experienced in many years, he says, not since school, he says, and even then, he got used to the bullying and built in some kind of cerebral coping mechanism. He was bullied a great deal. "A lot," he says, with some consideration. "You could even say I was something of a connoisseur of bullying."

The dog, the one that was put down in the vet's, it had rectal cancer, which is not good news for any species. Lewis's words. But Cliff can't tell if he's trying to be funny or just making an observation. Regardless, it sends him off in another direction, a consideration of the afterlife, and that it is strange we push the idea on our young that dead pets go to farmyards or petting zoos in the sky where they can enjoy running in fresh air in verdant fields for all eternity which is a peculiar model when you think of the tapestry of afterlife philosophies and if some culture somewhere believes we all go to our petting zoo equivalents, as humans, like do you think that's where your mother went, for instance, to some communal knitting parlour or Bingo Hall or whatever it is she enjoyed doing and not to mention some dogs just like lying on the rug in front of the fireplace but you never hear the story proposed of dead dogs going to the most comfortable rug in the universe in front of an eternal fire some of them you know like kibble and abhor exercise especially by the time they are old and die.

"What did you say about my mother? You said something about my mother."

Lewis's eyes flick his gaze around the auditorium. For the first time, he looks as if he's actually in the same dimension as Cliff.

He presses Lewis again.

"In these notions of the afterlife we were discussing, it seemed pertinent to use your mother as an example as she died quite recently, didn't she?"

"Don't talk about my mother."

Sammy is back, breaking the silence, and Rana is with him.

"We can't get hold of Preston," he says, and Cliff exhales and his shoulders drop. "But Rana has the number for an associate of Preston. Maggie someone?"

Cliff exhales again and says that Maggie won't have the film. He looks at his watch and does the math. "Plus, isn't it 7am in the UK right now?"

Sammy shrugs, looks at Rana for confirmation as he speaks, says, "She has a *version*, I am told. It is our best option at the present time."

"A *version*? What does that mean?" says Cliff.

"An edit," says Sammy. Sammy puts his large hand on Cliff's shoulder and says, "There is no need to worry, Robert."

"So, what does she mean by *an edit*?" Cliff says. "Because *AN* edit doesn't sound like *MY* edit."

Sammy takes his hand away.

"That, I do not know," he says.

There are a few moments of weighted painful silence, and then Cliff says, "Okay, well, I guess it will be good to have a back-up just in case the worst happens, and we can't get hold of Preston. A Plan B."

Sammy gives a nod and Rana goes off back to the office. Lewis's eyes are still wide and flickering around the place. Cliff sighs. He shouldn't have snapped at Lewis over his mother. Sammy, sensing tension, puts his arms around them both and says, "You must be hungry." It's barely an hour since breakfast. Cliff is not hungry. "Come on, I have some time before my next meeting; I'll take you both to this excellent little place for some *koshari*."

Lewis doesn't remember a great deal about growing up in Germany although he is aware of the manifesting legacy of his unorthodox childhood. His mind sometimes fizzes with images. Lens-flare images of his toddler self bumbling across a lawn in buckled shoes. He is twenty-five now, and he contemplates often the effect that spending his formative years on a barracks must have had on him, and not just that, but spending those years as the child of the ranking officer of that barracks, as if isolation can be compressed the further into the dungeon you travel. It's also worth mentioning that such a life removes you from much of the experience of living in a foreign country, and Germany was distant, and as he remembers it, remained largely unexplored. But what would have been the German culture he could have experienced anyway? He was eight years old when they left, it should be noted. But he would like to squeeze the experience out of him, like toothpaste from a tube, at some point, for a script.

Cliff isn't looking at Lewis as he speaks, but Lewis is looking at Cliff.

Sammy is a few yards ahead, having been accosted by one of his staff who is discussing something with him as they walk. It is a bright day, and the breeze has gone but the pleasant warmth remains, a little more humid now. The conference centre is outside of the city, off the highway, and beyond the gates of the compound is nothing, just a flat sandy horizon. They turn a corner onto a wide thoroughfare. Crowds of people bustle between stalls and at the end of the road is an empty stage at the back of which a screen, forty-foot high, blasts an Arabic music video channel through stacks that drown out all crowd noise. The music, loud enough as it is, but recorded in the red and so distorted and gravelly, takes Cliff's breath away even from half

61

a mile down the thoroughfare. Sammy looks back at Lewis and Cliff over his shoulder, offers that proud conspiratorial smile of his and ushers them forward with him. Cliff is trying to remember what *koshari* is. He knows he has had it before. There is a north-African restaurant just a few streets away from his house. The music is so loud, he feels himself wince. Lewis has not winced. His voice has gone up a notch, though.

He is saying that culturally perhaps he is a little lost, lost in the woods, which seems to have a Germanic element to it, a wandering star, which is a bit more *Paint Your Wagon*, an intellectual Nomad, which paired with the wandering star feels like a reference to the nativity. And although Lewis is without doubt the product of an international, itinerant upbringing, he feels he has not really experienced much of the world. His mild obsession with Japanese culture is dominated by the irony that he has never been there, and although it remains an ambition, it is something of a dream i.e. something he feels is unlikely ever to be realised. Cliff wonders why he doesn't just ask his father for the money to go on a trip. Or get a credit card. Poorer people than Lewis have gone to Japan for a month. And then Lewis says he would need a travelling companion to go to Japan, as he gets very anxious when outside of his comfort zone, and Cliff feels a dryness come to his mouth.

"The problem is," Lewis says, "is that I am a man who tends to talk too much."

Cliff stops.

Lewis stops too, completely unaware of why they have stopped.

Sammy and his employee continue to walk. Cliff recognises the need to keep up with Sammy and not lose him in the crowd. He starts up again and Lewis does too and he also starts talking again, as if his mouth is controlled by his feet, about how trying Egyptian cuisine will be interesting to him because, as he said, although he is the product of an international itinerant upbringing he has remained quite untouched by foreign cultures and that one day he will make a film about this. There is a manga artist who has done something similar with Japan's relationship with the United States.

Cliff takes a deep breath as there's little else to do with the air that just accumulated in his chest and shoulders.

Sammy has turned. "What is going on? You English are so slow."

"It's my fault," says Lewis. "I talk too much."

Cliff feels his eyebrows rise up. He's said it again.

Sammy laughs loudly, he leans back and opens up his frame.

"You don't talk too much," he says.

Cliff winces.

"We Egyptians," says Sammy, "*we* talk too much." He laughs again. "You have hardly opened your mouth the whole time you've been here. Who tells you you talk too much? We Egyptians, we talk talk talk talk talk talk talk talk. My wife says, Sammy, all you do is talk talk talk talk talk talk."

The word begins to lose its meaning.

It is hieroglyphics now.

At the far end of the thoroughfare is a car park. The man with Sammy points into a crop of 4x4s.

"We will go to this special little place downtown," Sammy says. He glances at his watch. "We have time."

Cliff decides, there and then, that the way to make a success of this day will be through willpower, and maybe that alone. He's not going to let it slide, watch it slip down the embankment and into a river of missed chances. He's going to give this his all.

They walk with a new determination, all four of them, into the melee of trucks and people carriers and off-road vehicles, like bank robbers embarking on a job, heads down, serious looks, Lewis following them like a post-punk C-3PO.

Cliff thinks of his film, stranded on a hard drive in London somewhere. He looks at his own watch. It's too early for Preston to be in the office. In fact, it's a Friday, and he may not make it in at all. He likes his routine; his rituals. Friday mornings Preston takes a breakfast meeting at the Italian place across the street from his office on Denmark Street. Always does. Invents a reason for a meeting if one isn't imperative. And then, depending on how long that goes on for, he either strolls across and picks up his messages, or goes directly to get his table in Molly's as close to noon as possible. Preston will not answer his mobile phone unless it's absolutely vital that he does so and he's expecting the call. The fact he has a phone at all is no small thing. His PA convinced him to have one, and she put her number in it before showing him how to use it. Preston is sixty-two years of age and wears his toupée as lightly as he does his cufflinks and spray tan. His PA, Beryl, is older than him. She wears frilled collars and has a rotary dial phone on her desk. Preston's offices have been pushed further and further out of the mind of Soho, if not the postcode, over the years; he's retained in his person and in his office the seedy charms of the place as it once was. Cliff doesn't know Preston all that well, but he knows his routines. It was gone over in great detail in Preston's self-published autobiography, *With These Proud Feet: The Story of Preston Proudfoot.* Cliff read the print-on-demand copy Preston gave to him, convinced it was a condition of the investment. Later Cliff realised the £24.99 retail price had been knocked off Preston's investment into *The Last January.* Had Preston actually said, "I only invest in ideas that truly know me"? Or had Cliff imagined that as something typical of him to say? One memory was clear, at the base end of desperation in the quest for that final piece of the financing puzzle, Cliff was going to do whatever it took. To coax money from this man, Cliff would have to go hell for leather worshipping at the temple of Preston. It's true: there was nothing he wouldn't do to get his movie made. But eleven hundred single-spaced glossy pages of A4, with a promised quiz at the end before any name was put on any dotted line, was as tough as it got.

Strange how it had come in handy, then, all that engorged prose intercut with peculiar dead-eyed data dumps of his daily routines, presumably dumped in place of the wisdom pearls of entrepreneurial success. Moneymen always seem to believe their moneymaking skills are part of their DNA, part of their make-up, and so, rather than advice on how to hire a good accountant (Preston would brag he hadn't paid a penny in tax since Wilson was Prime Minister), or how to invest inheritance (Preston set up his first company at the age of eighteen with a £20,000 starter fund from his father in 1971), the book is filled with sage ruminations on hearty breakfasts, rounds of golf, and generous philandering. Cliff read it all, felt his eyeballs melting with every turned page, felt himself getting stupider with every dry anecdote. But now, these few years later, he knew that Rana would not get hold of Preston this early on a Friday morning.

"Shouldn't we be keeping an eye on the progress of my film?" Cliff says.

Sammy lifts his phone and waves it as he lights a cigarette.

"Rana will keep me in the loop," he says.

"I just feel I would be better off if we were there, with Rana, getting this resolved. Making sure."

Sammy waves his phone again, takes a deep drag on his cigarette. Both items look dainty in his big meaty hands, like playing cards at the start of a trick.

They drive for fifteen minutes. Cliff adopts his usual position when visiting foreign cities; his nose to the window, the one-second snaps of new lives drifting past. Cairo is clean, there are few pedestrians, at least on this route; the traffic busy but not bumper-to-bumper like some places he's been – Mumbai, Kolkata, L.A., New York, Tokyo. Cairo seems less loud, less frantic. What are his touchstones for this city? Cliff did little research before coming. There wasn't much time, he told himself now. This wasn't like other cities he'd visited in recent years, places where the destination was part of the project. The project in this case was already complete. In all honesty, Cliff had given the city of Cairo very little thought. It brought with it ideas of prestige, of glimmering glamour, of millionaire boats in sparkling nightlife on the waterways of the Nile; a Cannes with the added gravitas of ancient stone. All a bit dreamy, vague, and probably more connected to the advertisements of Dubai he'd watched in the tiny televisions of Emirates Airways flights. The Arabia of jewels and broad white smiles. But now, as it goes past the window of Sammy's 4x4, he allows Cairo to have its say. What had this most ancient and glorious of cities impressed on him in his short life? He thinks about it. First thing that comes to mind is a sensation, one of coolness in a flurry of oppressive heat, and one of dirt being washed away, new life, new hope. Is it to do with the cycle of the Nile, the revivifying flow of the great river, the flood-and-retreat-and-flood? Is it to do with the ancients' belief in the afterlife? All those famous monuments and mausoleums, great kings and queens buried with their servants so they didn't have to wipe their own bottoms after death? No, it isn't that. Cliff tries to go deeper, find the source. And, yes, predictably, there it is. *Lawrence of Arabia*. Peter O'Toole leading the Arab boy into the officers' club for a glass of beer. The cool marble floors, the palm fans. O'Toole walks past the billiard table and the officers in their long socks stop and stare at this Victorian ghost, his robes billowing, dirty from the impossible journey he's just made. *Lawrence of Arabia*. That's what Cliff has. *Lawrence of fucking Arabia*. Great movie, but it feels somewhat cheap for it to be the first thing that comes to him. Peter O'Toole, with those marble blue eyes. Cliff read a book about T.E. Lawrence. Years ago. Cliff was bed-ridden with flu and it was the only thing within arms' reach. Holed up in a girlfriend's flat in his early twenties, unable to summon the energy to get the bus home. A week on his back, delirious, reading about Lawrence's sadomasochism. Strange how that's all he remembers of the book now. That and the fact Lawrence died in a motorcycle accident after the war, but he knew that anyway; it opens the film. Lawrence had a thing for handsome young men. Cliff remembers the book said he "fell in love with them". He's not sure you'd get away with such soft euphemisms nowadays. No wonder Lawrence felt the boy deserved a beer.

They don't get stuck in traffic. Not once. The 4x4 moves smoothly, honestly, through the subdued waves of cars, a calm sea of metal, chrome, and glass; no bumpers get near any other bumpers, there is no sign of tempers fraying, not a single wagged finger, none of that regular feeling common in other big cities, the feeling Cliff had taken to calling "trafficular oppression" or "car syndrome". As for Sammy and his driver/friend, they mutter to each other in Arabic a few times. There is something close about them, something beyond the employer/employee dynamic, something affectionate, familial perhaps. Sammy has the dominance, but it's soft power, there's respect moving in both directions. Sammy is respected by all those who work for him, that much is quite obvious even from the introductions in the office that morning; but there is something more, a bond that works both ways. Maybe it's a family business? That would fit the vibe Cliff has been getting. Rana works for her dad, after all. Cliff wants to ask, as he watches the two in the front seats exchange short phrases closed off and hushed. But in the small space of the 4x4, it's Sammy's energy that dictates the direction of conversation. Sammy is a raconteur and he speaks with inflection; the stories come out of his chest with some depth, some character, some variance in pace. He belly-laughs infectiously. Just being in conversation with him is an invitation to an act of athleticism, a greased wrestle. Cliff looks at Lewis, and then he looks at Sammy and the driver, and he feels like he wants to climb over the gear stick and huddle between the two, leaving Lewis in the back on his own. The young man at the wheel operates it with a relaxed focus, somewhere between slumped *to* and embedded *in* his position. He is inured to Sammy's energy, he smiles and nods occasionally; he is there to drive the show, not take part in it.

"I set up my company twenty years ago," Sammy says, and he waves his large hand over to his left. "Our offices are down there." He says a few words in Arabic Cliff presumes to be a street name. "A very famous street in Cairo. A prestigious spot," he says, and smiles back at Cliff and Lewis. "I was a filmmaker," he says. He beams with pride. "Making movies is not a young man's game, but it was for me. The kind of movies I made, they were all about the energy and the intensity. Of the city. Of its people. Young love affairs. Fights. Politics. Rage. Passion. In the end I had to settle down. I made a very small mark as a young man, but I realised that working this way, creating these films, they were all-consuming and not good for the soul. When you're young, the soul can take it. You have time over life to win back what you have sacrificed. And you have more battery power in you when you are young, am I right?" He looks at Lewis but not at Cliff. "But that sort of thing is not so good for family, and in the end, you have to decide who you are. I don't think a man should look foolish if he can help it. So, I decided that my future was in helping others have their say. There is ego, of course there is. We all have it. All us men." He looks at Cliff and not at Lewis and then he laughs that belly laugh. "I think of the musician. A musician is all about the ego. Look at me on the stage, listen to my songs that are all about myself. I love you why don't you love me? Blah blah blah. A filmmaker should not be like that. He should explore the world, not himself. And by exploring the world he *learns* about himself. And as he does, so does the audience. Anything other is foolishness. We expect that of our youth. Foolishness. Although I have more respect for the young now than I ever did when I was one of them. Some are selfish. But here the majority are not like that. Very few are. Some are all about the ego. Some are lazy and ruled by the insular thoughts of their own minds. But many old men are like that too. We say they cannot grow up. But I think it is more than that. Some men just see only themselves no matter their age. They have small worlds. Me me me. But the youth I know now – many are great people." He lays a heavy meaty hand on the shoulder of his driver. "It is the youth who change the world. They are the ones without jaded souls. I left writing and directing because many years ago I turned thirty and realised I was better placed to help a thousand others. And that is how we change the world. Change landscapes, flood them with the waters of youth. *You* understand!"

It isn't clear this time whether he is directing this to Lewis or Cliff; Sammy doesn't turn, just glares into the rear-view mirror, his eyes sinister in the letterbox edit.

"Couldn't agree more," Cliff says, although he is immediately hit by the fact that he's not currently practising whatever it is that Sammy is preaching.

"I don't have a jaded soul," Sammy goes on. "But I would do now if I had carried on with my little films, trying to tell my little stories. We would go around with our cameras trying to get that all-important shot." His voice turns wistful. "Just over here, I remember it like it was yesterday, we danced between cars as my camera chased my protagonist through the city as he searched for his love." Sammy beams. "We could have died. Bang. Hit by a truck. And they wouldn't have stopped. Not back then. Different now. People have more time. Time to stop."

Cliff thinks about his film, shot mostly in a suburban semi-detached in Shepperton, with the climax taking place in the front garden, the protagonist on his knees looking to a blue sky of wispy clouds.

He glances back out the car window to the city. Cairo looks relaxed. It's laid back, easy, it leans into its stride, just as Sammy does when he walks.

"It is different for you, in the West," Sammy says.

"I suppose it is," says Cliff, wanting to be agreeable, but also not wanting to get too deep into a conversation about cultural frictions.

"Here, and in other Arabic nations, we look to our elders for wisdom, but to our youth to change things. Some of us do, anyway." He laughs and his eyes glisten with an exuberant charm. "Some are rightly terrified of the youth." He laughs. "It is almost a self-destructive streak. We lure our young into revolutionary thinking. Sometimes I wonder if we are even aware we are doing it."

"It is an act of regeneration," says Cliff, almost surprised he said it. He acts as if he had thought it all through, but in fact he is trying to understand what he meant, searching into the uncharted repercussions of statements like this in foreign places. Is there something in that short sharp sentence that could dig something up, cause offence?

Sammy is nodding to himself.

"And you'd think for Cairo, the oldest city in the world, that is something ironic, yes?" Sammy says.

Cliff and Sammy share a look. Sammy turns, strains to see Lewis behind him.

"What do you think?" Sammy says.

Lewis's eyes cast around the cabin of the 4x4 as if looking for a way out, an ejector button or something.

Eventually, he says, "Regeneration is where the art is. Like Bowie."

Cliff isn't sure whether comparing the revolutionary spirit of the Arabic Nations to the transition from Aladdin Sane to Ziggy Stardust is the ambassadorial subtlety that is called for in this exact moment, and he watches the air between Lewis and Sammy fizzle for a few seconds.

And a few seconds more.

Is Sammy getting angry?

Or is he thinking it over?

And then his face emerges into a wide grin.

"Revolution is art," he says. "I like this."

Sammy says something in Arabic to his driver, perhaps translating the phrase, and they both begin nodding and smiling. They exchange some more phrases, seemingly unpacking Lewis's pearls of wisdom.

Sammy turns back to Lewis.

"You like Bowie?" he says.

"Who doesn't like Bowie?" Lewis says coldly.

Sammy shrieks. It catches Cliff off guard – Lewis too – and they both jump, their eyes flicker.

"Favourite album?" Sammy says.

Cliff waits for it. He looks at Lewis. It'll be one of the Berlin albums.

Lewis puts his finger to his chin, like a child in a nativity play directed to THINK.

Berlin. Cliff would put his house on it.

"I think for sheer fusion of soulful enjoyment and electronic experimentation it would have to be *Low*."

Cliff nods to himself.

Sammy rolls his shoulders.

"I love *Low*," he says, with a disconcerting seriousness delivered in a low voice. "Such control. I admire things that bump up against my own nature."

Cliff catches this. He finds it very difficult to imagine Sammy is not utterly in control at all times.

"What about you, Robert?" Sammy says. "You like Bowie?"

"Of course. Big fan."

He is. He isn't lying. But he's somehow made it sound peculiar, unimportant, deferential, like Do you like Italian food? *Sure.* Shrug. *Whatever you say.*

"And do you have a favourite album?"

Cliff doesn't spend any time thinking about this, mainly because he knew it was coming.

"It depends what mood I'm in," he says. "I love *Young Americans.* But it would have to be the reissue and not the original which doesn't have 'Somebody Up There Likes You' on it. It's probably *Station to Station* overall. But really anything between seventy-two and eighty-four is fine by me. His best – if you want to be objective and think in terms of his songwriting – is *Hunky Dory*; but songwriting is not all Bowie is about, is it?"

Has Sammy stopped listening?

He's faced front, is nodding slowly with his bottom lip curled.

And then he says, "Revolution is art."

I'm always crashing in the same car.

"I can see it now," says Sammy, and he prods his friend on the elbow and repeats himself in Arabic. "Art that inspires and galvanises." Sammy goes on in Arabic, as if trying out an idea with his compatriot before presenting it to the two in the back in English. "That bolt of lightning. It is iconic. So powerful. Perhaps what we need in this city is something like that, a symbol for us all to get behind." Sammy twists in his chair. "You should meet some friends of ours," he says to Lewis. Sammy looks at Cliff as something of an afterthought.

"Shouldn't we get back to make sure my movie is making its way over to us?"

Sammy waves his hand.

"I tell you it will be fine. My friends: they are thinkers. Young revolutionaries. Not jaded like me."

Sammy is anything but jaded.

"I always like to meet new people," Cliff says, about to segue into a fuller explanation of why he would be more comfortable back at the conference centre looking over Rana's shoulder.

"Your film will be with us soon," Sammy says, as if anticipating Cliff's next sentence.

"Yes, I know," Cliff says. He wants to display confidence in Sammy as somehow he feels now anything else is some kind of lack of trust in Egypt itself.

"And we will have this food," Sammy says. "And *then* we can go back to the office and check on the film. We will put your mind at rest, Robert. And I have a meeting. And then we go and meet my friends. *Our* friends." He strikes the driver across the shoulder. "Our friends."

Cliff watches them both. Sammy and his driver exchange a glance.

The car has been quiet for a while. Sammy has his head bowed to his phone. He has excused himself. Something needs his sign off. Work-based WhatsApp.

The moment Sammy's head comes up, Lewis speaks.

"It's interesting that you focus on Bowie's lightning bolt. More accurately the symbol of Aladdin Sane. I use that symbol in the storyboarding for my script."

"You storyboard too?" says Sammy, apparently overjoyed by this revelation.

"It is the lightning bolt which facilitates the sea monsters to arise into the sand dunes. It is a direct reference, of course, to Lovecraft's use of meteorological phenomenon that he would have not understood on a cosmological level to raise the Ancients, and specifically Cthulu, from the nether-regions."

"My friends will find you most interesting," Sammy says.

"These friends," Cliff says, sliding into a brief pause in the conversation. "You say they are revolutionaries. In what sense are they revolutionaries?"

"Of the mind," says Sammy, as if this answers all questions.

"Yes, of the mind," says Cliff. "But are they also *of the body?*"

Sammy looks back at Cliff.

"You seem worried, Robert?"

"I'm not worried. I just have some questions."

"Before you get yourself worked up about it…"

Sammy raises a finger in the air which stops all talk, and he puts his phone to his ear. He talks quickly in Arabic.

Cliff looks at Lewis. Lewis remains impassive, the eyes and mouth of a man utterly unaware of what is going on, what is unravelling, potentially, for him. Cliff thinks of Preston's words. *Babysit.*

But Cliff has nothing to say. He's thinking on it, but he has nothing immediately. And then Sammy hangs up. And all he says is "Good" to himself.

"Sorted," Sammy says back to them.

Sorted.

That's all there is to know.

"It's been a long time since any of you guys *needed* a revolution," Sammy says after a brief pause.

It's a diversion tactic. Cliff recognises it straight away. Sammy, Cliff is learning, doesn't waste his time spent with people; small talk is not small talk, idleness is not idleness. It is all part of a bigger structure, leading to a palace of probability.

"I mean *the West*," Sammy says. "You Europeans. You don't go in for revolutions."

"I may disagree on whether we *need* one, Sammy," says Cliff. "But you're right, it's been a while since we had one."

Even as Cliff is saying this, he is worried he is forgetting an important local moment in recent history. Yugoslavia; was the war in the Balkans recent? Does that count? And is this the place to contradict a man when he is philosophising to his guests, in his own car, when he is about to pay for lunch?

Cliff glances over to Lewis, who offers him nothing back in return; Lewis doesn't even look back at him, even though he must feel Cliff's eyes on him at that close quarter.

"The West knows nothing of these civil wars," Sammy says, his tone dropping to a serious one.

Cliff gives himself a moment to see which way this will go. Will he say Yugoslavia?

Well, there is Yugoslavia.

Maybe too blunt.

Well, there is Yugoslavia, but I think in modern terms it is the exception that proves the rule.

But *is* it?

Does it prove the rule?

"Poll Tax," Sammy says. "Riots in London in protest against the Poll Tax."

Yes, damn, Cliff had forgotten about that.

But was that, technically, a revolution? Sammy is in charge of definitions, it seems.

"That could be the exception that proves the rule," Sammy says.

Cliff pinches his own leg, twists the skin in a sharp swift movement, annoyed he didn't say what was in his head. Always trying to please, to further soften and ease the path of least resistance, deferring to the tone of the room, don't contradict, a crippling need to make people feel comfortable. Even when the stakes were this low, just a light conversation about European revolutionary zeal.

Cliff winces.

It always came back to him, that moment from his past, one of a select few he carried with him wherever he went. London. Premier. Some guy – a distributor, a producer? – he said…

Of course, we all know why Avatar 2 isn't going to get made.

The man seemed to lean forward and backwards at the same time, and he mouthed…

The Jews.

Cliff was confused. He'd never met an anti-Semite before. The man grinned – *did he wink?* – as if they were bonded by this knowledge through the looking glass. Cliff felt a little sick, but he smiled back, felt more sick for doing so, and crunched down on the ice from his drink, hoping a splinter of the ice might pierce the roof of his mouth and give him an excuse to run off to tend to the wound.

That's deeply offensive. Ah yes, Marie was there. She didn't let it go. She told the man he was a *fucking slimeball*.

I'm glad you spoke, Cliff said to her later. *Better coming from you.*

The double cowardice.

Why is he thinking of this now? That one moment had scarred him. Scarred him but not bettered him. Was he supposed to be defending *The West* now? Arguing that white Europeans had just as much passion in their bellies for the righteous cause of civil justice as any Arab nation?

There was something about Sammy, the way he spoke about Egypt, about Cairo, it was etched with pride that felt to Cliff like it was correct, justified, organic. What did Cliff have? Awkwardness.

"The West isn't interested in Arabic cinema," Sammy says.

Cliff doesn't disagree with him. Lewis isn't engaging either.

"It would be good if we could help make that change," Cliff says.

Sammy nods.

"Your movie," Sammy says. "Small. All filmed in one house."

"In and around, yes." He is clinging to the scene in the front garden.

"About family. About love and loss."

"And other things, yes."

"Rana said it was a very beautiful movie about your mother."

"And other things, yes. She is kind to say it's beautiful."

"Heart. It sounds like it has heart. You can build a revolution with heart."

"I'd imagine that's a vital ingredient, yes."

Cliff isn't sure where this is going.

"*You* should meet my friends too. This afternoon."

"I thought I was already coming along?"

"Yes, you were. But maybe I could introduce you as a director?"

"As opposed to?"

"As opposed to Lewis's friend."

Sammy twists his waist and looks at Lewis, who is skimming through something on his tablet.

Cliff holds back as best he can from showing on his face the disdain for the last couple of exchanges.

"Your friends are interested in meeting filmmakers?" Cliff says.

"I have been trying to convince them that they need to frame their message in a way that will reach out further, that will be accessible to a wider audience."

"What is their message?"

"You will see."

Cliff now has a vision in his mind. An underground bunker with damp stone walls, and a group of student revolutionaries crowded around a table poring over pamphlets and maps and manifestos printed on the press one of them stole from the university. There are a few young men, mostly dashing, albeit in different ways, serious and tight, and the women, just as serious, the more vocal of the group, a few berets, lots of smoking, disagreements about the directions of things, all about the levels of radicalism. And there is Sammy, the elder, allowed in out of respect for his devotion to the cause, on the outskirts, and he says that the group needs to hone its message, and to hire a filmmaker to make a movie about the struggle and then that can get out on Netflix or Amazon or something and then it will *trend* as other students and bedroom radicals around the world will begin to tweet about the movie.

Yes, Cliff thinks; this is not a bad idea from Sammy.

But Sammy's not being heard.

He circles the group. He knows who has sympathies for his old ways. Mahmoud. The handsomest of the gang, keen eyes and a five o'clock shadow. Mahmoud says, You know Sammy is right. Let him bring his filmmaker here and then make up your minds. This could be a world revolution, not just one in the world's oldest city.

Cliff is still not sure if that's true.

Is Cairo the world's oldest city?

It sounds convincing.

He will Google that next chance he gets.

Mahmoud adjusts his beret and takes a thoughtful toke on his cigar. He calls to the others and tells them to listen, that they owe Sammy a debt of gratitude for that thing he did in that place that one time that meant none of them went to jail. One of the women explains that this is corporate revolution, and that by exchanging the governance of an autocrat for the platforms of silicone valley technocrats they are just creating more problems for themselves. Sammy explains this is about using the tools of the ruling elite to bring about change for the working classes. Many in the room are unsure. But they all remember that thing he did once in that place that one time that meant none of them had to go to jail, and they all begin to nod. They embrace him. One by one.

"You find money with ease for your movie in the UK?" Sammy says to Cliff.

"Christ no," says Cliff, and he lets out an alarming and involuntary snort. "It was very hard."

"If it is hard, you must be good at getting it, no?"

"That's one way of looking at it."

And Cliff had never looked at it that way before. He thinks about it for a moment. Maybe he *is* good at it.

"And Preston; what is he like?"

Cliff has to be careful. He looks at Lewis who is making patterns on his tablet screen with his thumb-tip and forefinger.

"He is old school. Do you say that here?" Cliff says. "You don't see many doing business like he does. He doesn't work in that corporate way. He doesn't have that mentality. As a partner, he is looking to see what pleasure he can get out of a deal. It doesn't have to be about any corporate mission statement, if you see what I mean?"

Cliff isn't sure Sammy does understand.

"I heard my uncle once paid a bar owner's tax bill in return for sex with his wife," Lewis says.

Sammy turns heavily in his seat.

Cliff is frozen to the spot.

Lewis does not look up from his tablet.

Sammy shrugs.

He says, "My advice to you, Robert, is to always know who it is you're going into business with."

What can Cliff say to that? That he was so desperate to get his film financed, and so many others had closed doors to him, that he was left with only two options: Preston or no movie. So, was he to reveal himself naïve or immoral? He's pretty sure Sammy would have no time for naïveté. What Cliff had shown in getting his movie financed was bloody grit and determination, that's what that was. It should be a tick in the pro column for Robert Clifford as a filmmaker. A guy who gets things done.

Cliff shifts a little awkwardly in his seat.

"In my experience, Preston is something of an old rascal nowadays, and nothing more troubling than that," Cliff says. "And who knows where these other stories come from. We all make enemies along the way, don't we?"

"I try not to," says Sammy.

Sammy is chewing something over.

"So, you have a good relationship with Preston?" Sammy says.

The atmosphere in the car seems to have loosened up.

"We seem to work well. He gives me my freedom, and I know how to get around his idiosyncrasies."

Cliff glances at Lewis, who is head bent to his tablet. In his relief, Cliff may have accidentally overshot in the last remark.

"And he will be interested in investing in your next film?"

"That depends," Cliff says.

"On what?"

"On how this one does, primarily."

Sammy is facing front, hasn't looked back at the two of them in a while.

"And what is the criteria for success?"

"Oh, the usual measurements. Box office. Territory distribution. Festival uptake."

"Prizes?"

Cliff looks hard at the back of Sammy's head, burrowing his vision into the hard space behind his right ear.

"A prize here or there certainly wouldn't hurt."

"This place has changed a great deal since the revolution," Sammy says as the car turns into Tahrir Square.

Traffic density increases but is still civil, and as they join the flow Cliff begins to see how some of the buildings at the perimeter are under renovation, some under reconstruction, and one soon-to-be-hotel is being erected behind billboards. He thinks about what he knows of what went on here, watched from the comfort of a damp flat above a charity shop where he lived at the time.

"You call it a revolution?" Cliff says.

"Vehemently," Sammy says vehemently.

"I think we called it a *Spring*," Cliff says half-remembering.

Sammy nods. Cliff looks at the back of his head, that hard point behind Sammy's ear.

"They want us now to call it a *disturbance*," Sammy says.

By *they* it is obvious he means the government, the rulers, those in charge, but whether it's any more specific than this it's impossible to tell. Cliff tries to remember if Egypt has a king or a president or prime minister, or if it's Egypt that had the Shah, but then he remembers reading the Kapuscinski book when he was a student — was it called *Shah of Shahs*? — and he's reintroduced to an era in his life when he *knew* things and he found himself at the fork in the road where he almost took the road of a person who *knows* things and who moves in the circles peopled by *knowers of things*, but instead he ended up where he is, cadging money from a man like Preston Proudfoot to indulge himself in his movie about his own thoughts.

Cliff snaps himself out of that rabbit hole.

He remembers the Arab Spring being in Egypt and being here in Tahrir Square because that was the weekend he joined Twitter.

Twitter. Often referred to now as "the Wild West", but to Cliff it often felt more like a pitched battle, like one of those eighteenth- or nineteenth-century ones with the brass buttons and feathered hats and young boys tooting pipes and rattling drums until they were torn to shreds by cannonballs. The Wild West may have been lawless, but it had the ethics of progress. Although, yes, the bigotry was perhaps comparable. Who knows exactly how rough the Wild West was in that regard, really? Progress was made, and at a huge cost to ethics as well as lives. Twitter isn't like the Wild West at all, is it? It's different *and* worse. Nobody on Twitter is building a railroad or panning for gold. And on Twitter nobody could shoot you in the back, like what happened to Wild Bill Hickock. No. It's all up front. Who you are and who you were all in one twisted time continuum. And who are you on there? Who was Cliff in this new Wild West? Quite often just a drummer boy stuck in the mud.

Cliff had joined, behind the curve but only just, because his friends from school were communicating through it for free back when text messages still cost a pretty flash of silver per sentiment. He was out of the loop. That drove him mad. It's coming back to him now, as Sammy talks about the revolution. Cliff joined Twitter because he felt left out, but the first day he was on it, he ended up watching a building burn down in the heart of Cairo through a link to Al-Jazeera. He looks up. Was *that* the building? Or *that* one? Perhaps behind those billboards, a five-star hotel is rising from the ashes. Twitter back then had a pure function. One hundred and forty characters. You could argue about the accumulation of micro experiences all adding up to mean something, but without threads, without the ability to mangle fireworks out of additional functions, it was the words that meant something. Or maybe that's all bullshit. Maybe it was just as bad then. Who really remembers? But Cliff *does* remember reading a thread from a journalist that day who was tweeting from the back of a police van that was going around hoovering up writers off the street. Dissident suppression happening before his eyes and in real time. Did Cliff know this was a glimpse of the future, the future where nobody hides, where nobody dies alone? Something was obvious about it, even to him.

For the next twenty minutes, Sammy gives them a tour of the Square, the car making several circuits, and each circuit bringing new things.

"This is where the tanks sat," Sammy says, "and this is where the cobbles were awash with blood. Students. Young people."

He looks at them as if this was proof of what he had been saying earlier, that the young people would change the world and it had always been thus. Cliff isn't so sure of the argument as a broad statement of history, but there is something to Sammy's conviction that it's true that makes it powerful enough to carry weight.

Sammy goes on; his voice is unsteady for parts, a courageous tremble, some parts sorrow and some parts pride, and Cliff continues to look at the back of his head, the edges of a close haircut specked with salty white.

The car pulls up beneath a bridge.

Sammy nudges the driver, giving him some instruction in Arabic, and the driver takes out his phone.

"Hold it up," Sammy says.

The video is from a YouTube playlist. CNN. Aerial footage with the commentary removed. A thick grey snake of people advancing upon a retreating line of men in hi-vis jackets across a bridge, this bridge, the one above them. Cliff wouldn't have recognised it, a different day, a grey day, dusky, but he may have guessed, and anyway Sammy, wide-eyed, is pointing upwards with his forefinger.

"These are the pro-government faction, Mubarak's people." Sammy points to those retreating back into the traffic, trucks and cars that continue on their way as if nothing is going on. Rings of smoke from flung grenades, sparks of flames from Molotov cocktails.

"Nine years ago," Sammy says.

"Feels like yesterday," he says.

"Heroes."

Cliff can see Sammy's face now as he is twisted in his seat to watch the CNN footage alongside him and Lewis.

"The Ultras," he says. "We call them the Ultras, those who fought here for *our* freedom. The young men. They created a front line for the millions who prayed for freedom, and many of them died for us."

The air in the car changes, some ancient weight.

"My son," Sammy says. "He was seventeen."

Sammy turns back in his seat to face the front, and the driver, with a glisten to the corner of his eye, puts his phone back in his pocket.

"Your son was here?" Cliff says.

"He was an Ultra," says Sammy, "on that bridge." He points again upwards. "That is the last footage of him. Somewhere he is in that crowd."

Cliff looks at Lewis, who has been silent and still this whole time, and he is silent and still next to him now on the back seat.

"They said he fell," says Sammy. "Later that day. Hit his head on the curb. But he would not go so easy. Not my son."

It is a defiant sentence.

The driver adjusts the stick and the car moves smoothly back out into the steady flow of traffic.

"It is important always to educate people about what happened here," Sammy says. "Revolution. *Not* a disturbance."

The meal, at a bench and table at the roadside about five minutes' drive from Tahrir Square, is eaten with more relish than Cliff had anticipated; the noodles and rice and chilli paste and vinegar giving an acidity to the air between the four of them. Cliff wants to talk more about the Arab Spring, although he doesn't want to press on a subject that has at its centre, for Sammy, the death of his son. A bloodline to direct history, to violent uprising, to change. And Sammy would surely talk more given a nudge, his pride, the emotion, that is not something so easily suppressed. Lewis remains quiet as he eats. He seems to be enjoying the food, served up in a stocky round disposable dish with a wooden spork, but he is going at it like every mouthful is some new wonder. Sammy, it seems, is content with what went before, the educating of his guests as to what happened nine years ago. The Revolution. There is no obvious way to pull him back to it. Cliff lets it go.

The air is warm, and a light, refreshing mid-morning breeze moves through it and across their table.

"Your film is personal to you?" Sammy says to Cliff.

"Of course," says Cliff.

"It is about your mother?"

Cliff quickly chews and swallows the noodles in his mouth.

"Not really," he says as a waft of chilli paste hits the back of his throat. "Obviously, there is something in the character of the mother that draws on my own," he says, and his eyes begin to water, and he feels his throat go dry. He takes a sip of water.

But it seems to stoke some deeper fire. There's a chance a chilli flake, or a collection of them, have stuck to the wall of his throat.

Cliff begins to hiccup.

"Don't worry," Sammy says, and he begins to pat Cliff on the shoulder. "There is nothing to be embarrassed about. You should be proud that you made a film in honour of your mother. I am in awe of artists who can do things like that."

But it isn't about my mother.

Cliff can't say it, though. He is somehow currently defying many assumed biological conventions and simultaneously hiccupping *and* coughing.

Was that an inch of noodle that just came out of his nose?

Sammy is perhaps a little embarrassed for Cliff. He turns to Lewis. Gives Cliff some personal space in which to recover.

No wait. My movie is not about my mother.

Cliff's voice, so pleading, so weak, echoes in his own head but goes no further, does not reach his mouth. He splutters, coughs, tries to drink more water. His eyes stream.

The driver, eating with them, gets up and goes back to the kiosk.

"He will get you some yogurt," Sammy says. "It is best for that."

He points at his own throat but there is the touch of a smile to the edge of his mouth. Cliff waves in gratitude. *But the film is not about his mother.*

Sammy turns to Lewis.

Don't do it, Sammy.

Wait until I have my yogurt and we can continue our conversation.

Cliff cannot speak but he is watching them both now, a cup of water to his mouth.

"Lewis: tell me about your background," Sammy says.

A knife to the heart.

Cliff watches, listens, as Lewis begins a potted personal history and unfiltered memoir. It begins in Germany but runs into several self-explanatory subunits about the psychology of his father (again) but this time with some references to the cold loyalty of his mother, who, in Lewis's words, *strained* to love him. If Sammy feels uncomfortable with this psychoanalytical honesty, he doesn't show it. He furrows his brow, nods in what looks like sympathy. Lewis twists, leaps this way and that, and gets to Lovecraft once again, and postulates on the relationship Lovecraft had with his own mother and how it was most likely the root of his unpleasantness. Sammy nods.

"He is the one with the monsters under the ground?" he says. "Cthulu; is that right? Am I pronouncing that right?"

"That's right," Lewis says. "Not everybody gets that right. It's supposed Lovecraft wrote it to be unpronounceable."

They both laugh.

"I have seen it written down," Sammy says. "But never thought to say it out loud before. I was unsure."

They laugh again.

Cliff watches, his eyes moving between them, the cup of water up to his mouth.

"Do you believe in all that kind of stuff?" Sammy says.

Lewis frowns, and then laughs incredulously.

"Of course not," he says. "That would be absurd."

Sammy is smiling widely.

Cliff's hiccupping continues although the coughing has abated.

"Have you been to Guinea?" Sammy asks.

Did Sammy just cut Lewis off?

Cliff can't be sure from behind the cascading waters of his eyes. He blinks wildly and breathes shallowly.

Lewis says he has not been to Guinea, and Sammy frowns and says, "Then why have you set your script there?"

Lewis puts his hand to his chin and his eyes flicker in a pose of thoughtfulness and he says, "That's a very good question and one I'm not entirely sure I have a satisfactory answer for, but to say that when he retired my father bought a diamond mine there. My mother was certain it was because he was having an affair with 'a native', she said, and she became convinced he had sired an illegitimate child and although all of this was extremely dramatic she still refused to leave him or divulge the source of her paranoia if indeed it was paranoia but of course this could be a pertinent example of just because someone is paranoid doesn't mean they're not out to get you."

The yogurt is placed firmly in front of Cliff on the table in a small clay pot with a wooden spoon standing up in it.

It breaks the silence.

Cliff normally would have allowed the silence to linger, to see what comes out of it, to see what Lewis has left in him, but his throat is itching, his hiccups are raw, so he grabs the clay pot and begins shovelling helpings of yogurt into his mouth. The relief makes his eyes narrow.

The drive back to the festival site is in conversational silence. Sammy takes a call in the front seat and his hushed Arabic merges with the flut flut flut of tyres rolling on hot tarmac. Cliff notices that Lewis is writing something in the notes app on his phone, but he can't see what it is. Lewis frequently stops and stares into the middle distance, the back of the driver seat, before rejoining his note-making. He doesn't look out the window at the city going by, not once. Cliff has stopped feeling for a space to reignite the conversation about his movie being about his mother. He will do so later when he has Sammy's full attention. The time will come. Instead, he finds his thoughts not with Cairo, which passes by the window in rolls and waves, and they are not with his film, or even his mother, but, dammit, they are with H.P. Lovecraft and *his* mother. Is it true? Can a bad matriarchal relationship result in the child growing up to be a terrible person?

There was a party once, Cliff is now thinking of it. Maybe fifteen years ago. Halloween. He'd been thinking of costumes. He was leafing through the garments in his girlfriend's wardrobe for inspiration. Kelly. She was petite, but had a big smile, was punchy, had grown up with three brothers, and her style was a variety of flowing, billowing clothes, neo-hippie. She was a trainee nurse and smoked a lot of weed and she liked shoegaze bands, the only girl he had ever met who did. They had nothing in common, apart from the fact they never really fought, only play-fought, and that seemed to be enough at the time. And they had lots of uncomplicated, no-nonsense sex for the few months they were together. They liked to get hammered and watch horror movies and they always seemed to be sitting in the same booth at the pub. Entire weekends in that booth. He was going through her clothes rack and she came in and when he told her he was looking for a Halloween costume she didn't take it well, and she started battering him with a pair of jeans that he'd slung over the wardrobe door. As he cowered down the side of the bed, blows of jeans raining down on his raised forearm, Kelly began to laugh, and she got out of breath quite quickly and collapsed on the bed. "Cheeky motherfucker," she said. They both laughed until they were panting, and as things calmed, Kelly lifted herself up on to her elbow and looked at Cliff supine down the side of the bed. "You could go as the Mad Arab," she said. "Bit racist," said Cliff. "No, I mean the Mad Arab. He wrote the *Book of the Dead. The Necronomicon.* You know, from the *Evil Dead.*" Cliff looked at her like he didn't know what she was talking about. She hopped up off the bed and went to the wardrobe and began going through her own clothes and pulled out a few garish silk dresses. "I've done it before," she said. "I even have a turban-type hat in a box up there somewhere. What? You're looking at me like you don't have a clue what I'm talking about." But, yes. The Mad

Arab. Lovecraft's wizard who wrote the book of magic that summons the demons. Cliff stares out of the car window, half-sure the car will turn at any moment and there he will be, Abdul Alhazred on the pavement, chanting, his eyes rolled to white, luring a megalithic demon creature out of the depths and onto the street side. Cliff and Kelly spent hours wrapping Cliff in silks and darkening his eyes with liner, and blinging him up until he looked the very vision of an evil Arabian wizard. Inspired. Kelly? She went as a sexy witch.

Cliff looks over at Lewis, paused in one of his thoughtful moments staring at the back of the driver seat, his phone held up like a compass.

Cliff feels an urge. Something connected to what happened in Tahrir Square. It is peculiar. It's like fresh air. It's joyful.

"Can I read your script?" Cliff says.

Lewis's eyes sparkle.

He umms and uuuuughhhs, and he looks down at his bag at his feet and he says, "I don't have a copy."

"You *do* have a copy," Cliff says. "It's in your bag."

"That's not a *copy*," Lewis says. "That's the original. I mean, okay it is a copy of the original, but it is the only copy of the original I have here in this country, so it acts as an original, and I hadn't intended on really just handing it around to anybody."

"To *anybody*? I'm hardly anybody."

"Perhaps we could see back at Sammy's office if there's a way to print a real copy for you. I have it on my laptop. That would then be a copy. You could have *that* copy."

Cliff looks at him.

He has several ways he can take this, but which way is somewhat out of his control. He feels a rage building. That rage will be the judge. "Why can't I just read the copy in your bag?"

"As I said, it's not a copy, not really, not in the context of this trip."

"But I don't understand what the fear is. I'm sitting right here next to you. What is going to go wrong? Are you afraid some great bird will come through the window of the car and carry it off in his beak? Do you not want me to read it? You can just say if you don't want me to read it."

"No, you can read it if you want to by all means, I have no issue with you *reading* it, I just have this manuscript, the one in my bag, and that is for presenting to people here."

"I am here."

"But it is for people who make movies."

Silence.

The car is pulling into the conference centre complex. Sammy finishes his call.

"I could have just sat here and read the first few pages and given it back to you," Cliff says, looking out of the window. "No harm would have come to your script," he says.

"I can get you one printed, I'm sure, at Sammy's office if you really want to read it."

"It's not that I *want* to read it, Lewis." The car doors open in front. "I was offering to give you some feedback on it; help you out."

Cliff opens his door and gets out.

The last thing he sees of Lewis in the back of that 4x4 is a look of perplexity on his usually expressionless face.

Back in the office, both of them cupping paper beakers of steaming black tea, Cliff feels terrible about his outburst in the car. He leans and whispers to Lewis, "I'm really sorry if I snapped at you. It's probably the stress, y'know; everything going on with my film."

Lewis responds with a curt *hum*, and for a second Cliff is unsure what it means.

He stares at him, side-on. Was it an accepting hum, a dismissive hum, a hum that declares there was really no need for an apology in the first place and that he, Lewis himself, accepts some of the responsibility for luring Cliff into said snap with his frustrating and nonsensical attitudes toward the script?

"People don't usually apologise," Lewis says.

Cliff sits back on the chair and they are separated now by the foliage of a potted plant.

Everything is so much effort. Everything. Lewis was not supposed to change every colour of this trip. He wasn't supposed to *dominate* it. He is supposed to be an inconvenience thrust upon Cliff by one of his financiers. Cliff huffs, exhales forcefully, but manages to keep it quiet and Lewis can't see him from the other side of the plant. It feels good to exhale like that, like he's pushing out stale air.

He looks across the office at Rana and she catches his eye and offers Cliff a steady lingering smile. She is at her desk, phone to her ear, and when her smile fades it seems to take on more importance. Bad news? It is surely bad news. He smiles back, almost as if he can change the news by sheer will.

They are waiting – or rather Cliff is waiting with Lewis at his side – for a reporter from a national newspaper to come to the office to interview Cliff about his film. Sammy said with some pride that the film writers in Egypt are very passionate, very well-informed, and they will have in-depth questions.

"But they won't have seen the film," Cliff said.

Sammy patted him on the shoulder and said that they have a feel for these sorts of things, whatever that means.

"What do you think that means?" Cliff says to Lewis from behind the foliage. He is still watching Rana. She is no longer looking back at him. "Sammy said the journalists here have a *feel for this sort of thing*. What do you think that means?"

Lewis speaks from deep in the greenery. He does nothing to emerge. Cliff cannot see his face. "I've never done an interview," is all Lewis says.

Cliff shouldn't have snapped at him in the car. He sips his tea. It's still too hot, but he deserves the burning.

"That was quite an experience earlier," Cliff says into the leaves. It was time to try and ingratiate himself with Lewis, create some common ground. "Tahrir Square. I hadn't quite expected that when we got on the plane. A guided first-person tour of a major moment in history."

Silence.

"What did you think?" Cliff says.

Slowly, slower than usual, almost as if it is the result of evolving thought, Lewis says, "It felt voyeuristic."

Cliff hadn't been expecting that.

It makes him feel sad that Lewis feels this way, sadness tinged with the arsenic of anger, and for that second, he is glad the potted plant is between them.

Voyeuristic.

Nobody ever uses that word in a positive context. It's a word that gets under the skin, that worms its way into the bloodstream. It's sordid. And the insinuation that Cliff doesn't feel the same way means that he was absorbed by the voyeurism, did not question it, perhaps did not even recognise it, and so was something sordid, low, degenerate himself.

Voyeuristic.

But Cliff has done enough damage for one morning, and he refuses to be angry at Lewis twice. He shuffles a bit in his seat. It's not easy to give the kid this kind of break, but it is the right thing to do. "What do you think of meeting Sammy's friends later on?" he says.

"I must admit I wasn't really listening," says Lewis. "But they are producers."

Cliff isn't sure if that's a question or a statement.

"Are they?" he says.

"Yes."

"Because I didn't get that from what Sammy was saying."

"Yes. They are producers."

"What makes you think they're producers?"

"They want to meet me about my script idea."

"No; no, they don't."

Lewis peers at Cliff through the foliage.

"Why do you say that?" Lewis says.

"Because they're not producers."

"I took that they were producers."

"Maybe it was just a bit lost in translation."

Don't give the kid a hard time.

"How in translation? He was speaking English. And I speak English."

"It's a saying."

"Not an applicable one."

"I disagree. You misunderstood him. Lost in translation."

"I don't think you understand that phrase," Lewis says.

"Of course I understand that phrase. You're being too literal."

"Perhaps it's just lost in translation to *you*."

"Now you're making it obvious you don't understand the phrase."

"I understand the phrase," Lewis says. "And there was nothing to translate."

Cliff rubs his eyes with his thumb and forefinger.

"Anyway, that doesn't matter," he says. "I just think you've misunderstood what Sammy was trying to explain to you."

"It seems to me he wasn't trying to explain anything."

"But I don't think these friends of his are movie producers."

"Why else would they be interested in meeting me?"

"It seems a long way back up the track now, but it had something to do with David Bowie."

"David Bowie?"

"You said something about Bowie as an icon, and I think it struck a chord with Sammy."

"Bowie is a universal language."

"He is."

"Can't lose Bowie in translation."

"You're funny," says Cliff, half-exhausted.

"Did you know Bowie recorded a German version of 'Heroes'?" Lewis says.

"Yes."

"For the German market."

"Yes, I knew that."

"Helden."

"Yes. He also did a French version. Héros."

Cliff knows that Lewis is totally ignoring his contribution to this conversation.

"Some people think the German version is an example of Bowie's chameleon-like aptitude for taking on the colours of the environment around him. So, he was in Berlin, and learned German for that track. But I think it just shows he was smart enough to show respect to the German market. I lived there. I know they respond to that kind of thing."

Off topic. Way off topic. How does Cliff end up in these places?

"I just wanted to say I think we should be careful," Cliff says.

"Careful? Why?"

"We are here for one job. To present *my* film."

"I'm not."

Cliff thinks.

"No. I'm not sure why you're here, actually."

"To meet people."

"Yes; to meet people. But that doesn't mean *any* people."

"Producers."

"I don't think these people are producers."

"You don't *think*? You are less sure than you were a few minutes ago."

Cliff winces.

"I think Sammy wants you to meet some friends of his who may or may not be…" Cliff hasn't really thought about how he's going to put this. "…anti-establishment."

"They sound cool."

Wince.

"They most likely are, Lewis," says Cliff. "But that doesn't mean they will be good for your career."

"Or yours, for that matter."

"What does that mean?"

"Sammy wants you to meet them too."

"So, you understood *that*?"

"It was easy to understand. Sammy speaks good English and there is no danger of anything being lost in translation."

"Now you're misunderstanding *me*."

"It sounds like you want to meet them on your own."

"That's not what I meant."

"Are we in competition? Is that why you wanted my script?"

Cliff dips his voice into a strained, frustrated hush.

"I didn't want your script. I just offered to read it to give you a bit of feedback."

"Try and make it worse?"

"We're not in competition."

"I think that's a healthy attitude."

"It's not about having an attitude," Cliff says. "It's just what it is. It's what we are. To each other. We are not in competition and I recognise that fact. Not an attitude. A fact."

"So why try and dissuade me from meeting these producers?"

Wince.

Deep breath.

"I'm not trying to dissuade you. And they're not producers. I'm just asking you to think this through. We are not here to get mixed up in anything."

"Mixed up in getting my film financed."

"You think these guys are going to finance your film?"

"It looks like Sammy thinks they will finance yours."

Cliff's head is spinning. He has to think for a moment. That's not how it went.

"That's not how it went."

Cliff huffs.

Crosses his arms and looks across the office and calms himself down.

"I think Sammy believes his friends might make a good subject for a movie," Cliff says. "God only knows how much he's thought of this beyond that. I have a feeling. I have a feeling and I need to make sure I keep an eye on it. And the truth is your uncle Preston told me to look after you. So, that's what I'm trying to do. I didn't want the gig, but there it is. We are where we are. And if these guys Sammy wants us to come meet are some underground revolutionary group wanted by the authorities, I'm just saying we should maybe just make our excuses and give it a miss. I don't want either of us to get into trouble. Your script is no doubt great, and you'll have other opportunities."

Cliff looks at the potted plant. Lewis is quiet. Maybe he's taking this on board, thinking it through. Maybe Cliff is getting through to him finally.

Cliff leans forward. And peers around the front of the plant.

Lewis is on his phone. He has his headphones in.

One of the office workers comes over, a young woman whose headscarf gives the impression of a perfectly spherical face, like a plate with eyes, nose and mouth drawn on, and she smiles so warmly for a moment Cliff is transported, heated up from the inside, taken far away from Lewis. Cliff's mouth opens half an inch, expectantly, waiting for the information this delightful young woman is delivering, if indeed it's not Cliff himself she is to deliver from the dark thoughts Lewis inspires in him. If that is her mission, then so far she is doing a fine job of it. She leans in, the smile holds up, and she takes hold of the pot plant.

"This is in your way," she says. And she lifts it although it's six feet high and looks too heavy for her, and she carries it to the other side of the room.

Cliff can hear himself saying, *no no no don't worry, don't trouble yourself*. But that smile is solid, and she has pride in the small things she can do for others.

He can feel Lewis at his side, revealed like a pagan idol peeled out of the Aztec Amazon, before he turns to look at him.

Cliff swallows. Lewis has a look in his eye.

Lewis speaks.

"I was uncomfortable with it," he says. "It felt as if I was imposing on someone else's personal drama which is ironic for someone who *writes* drama and has written a script and will direct that script whilst carrying a great deal of personal material that has been and then will be transposed into drama for the world to see... I consider myself a *deconstructor* of narrative convention

rather than any sort of traditional *constructor*... monsters, creatures, transported back and forth through time loops... destroy the beginning, middle and, to a certain extent, ends... slowly devoured by it folding in on him... Breaking the fourth wall... admitting my own cowardice while still expressing my ideas... which perhaps brings us back in an inverted way both to the feeling of imposition on watching the personal story in the Square and the unpleasantness of Lovecraft's personality......
..............."

Cliff floats up and out of the office, across the mezzanine, and he lowers elegantly into the auditorium, levitating above the crowds who either do not see or choose to ignore him. He floats out of the conference centre, maybe through the roof of the building, it's difficult to tell, and he heads steadily at a leisurely glide toward the city. The sky is a brilliant clear cobalt, an occasional wisp of thin cloud gives the expanse some perspective. It's the most beautiful warmth, the most pleasant sort. From up here he can see what must be the whole of the city; and it is a stunning tapestry of sand-coloured buildings, terracotta rooftops, shining glass and palm leaves. And there, in the distance, not too far, he can see the unmistakable shape of the Pyramids of Giza. They don't quite look real. They look like discarded cardboard boxes. He thinks again of T.E. Lawrence and his penchant for beautiful young men. His sadomasochistic tendencies. Cliff allows himself a half smile and he closes his eyes to the light breeze. God, this is better than being present, he thinks to himself. Better than listening to Lewis.

There's a noise. Another presence.

From the corner of his eye, Cliff catches some commotion. Some smoke. A spark. He floats toward it at a gentle pace. It is the revolutionary confrontation on the bridge at Tahrir Square. The one that Sammy showed him on the CNN YouTube channel. The crowds jeer, the grenades smoke, the Molotov cocktails shatter into sprays of flame. He looks down on it all. Tanks begin to gather at the top of the north road. The crowd swells. Cliff feels nervous for them. The Ultras. They push forward, bottles crack on tarmac, stones fling, zip and ricochet along the road and off the side rails. Police with riot shields in formation begin to mount the bridge. From where Cliff is levitating, he can feel the wind pick up.

A helicopter.

It's up there with him just off to the left. It has the letters CNN painted along the side in meaty red letters. From an open door in its side, a man leans out and trains a television camera onto the bridge. The pilot locks aviators on Cliff; the two of them exchange an American-style snapped salute. They both, Cliff and the pilot, look back down at the bridge. The battle intensifies. Cliff looks back at the pilot, who gestures to him. Get in. Get in the chopper. Cliff figures why not, how long can he hang up here anyway? He front-crawls to the door and the cameraman helps him in with a tug of Cliff's belt. He pats Cliff across the shoulder as Cliff secures himself into the co-pilot seat and does up his safety harness. The pilot shakes him by the hand, taking a second away from the job of flying, and he points to the unused headset hooked over the co-control stick. Cliff puts them on.

"What are you doing up here?" says the pilot.

"It's a long story," says Cliff.

What is he doing up here?

The pilot looks back over his shoulder at the cameraman, who nods and says, "Five more minutes."

"I think I'm having some kind of out-of-body experience," Cliff says.

"Is that so?" says the pilot. "And what's brought that on?"

Cliff feels slightly drunk. Lightly drunk. Maybe it's the altitude, or the cold from flying in just slacks and a cotton shirt.

"I have this travel companion," Cliff says. "He's proving difficult. Maybe it's me. I don't know. But he is... how can I say this... it's like he exudes an ancient force, something from deep down in the mysteries of time. Incomprehensible. I can already see in your face you think I'm exaggerating." Cliff looks at his own reflection in the pilot's aviators. "And I don't blame you. I'd feel the same in your shoes. You think I must be short-tempered, intolerant. It's him you feel sorry for right now. I get that. I really do. But I do believe that if an aggressive government, like your government, the American government, like if the CIA got hold of him, my travel companion, they would modify him best they could and send him into combat situations. He could destroy armies. Destabilise economies. Overthrow dictators. Have dictators overthrow themselves. Do you know anyone in the CIA?"

The pilot says nothing. He is impervious behind those shades.

"Shame," says Cliff. "That's probably why I'm here, though, having this out-of-body experience."

"You think your body is there now?" says the pilot.

"Almost certainly," says Cliff. "I'm probably sitting there, nodding, offering the occasional yeah and the odd uhum. This is my safe space, up here. This used to happen when I was a kid."

"You used to fly?"

"Not necessarily fly. But I'd go elsewhere. Leave my body behind, go wandering. Lessons. Maths. You know, when I was about fourteen, I had a year-long love affair with Miss Jenkins the French teacher and she never even knew. I bought her flowers, we walked through the woods, we wined and dined. It was true love."

True love.

Cliff and the pilot look down onto the bridge. The tanks have rolled forward, and the Ultras are falling back. The noise rises, flames rise too.

"You getting this? Larry?" the pilot shouts above the noise of the rotor blades.

"In glorious Technicolor," Larry the cameraman shouts back.

They all watch a rush and a push.

"Can you fly?" says the pilot. "Like really fly? Not just pushing yourself around like you have been?"

"I can fly," says Cliff, "but I'm not a professional. I feel safer just levitating and watching."

"This is a beautiful city," says the pilot; "it's a shame you're not being allowed to enjoy it."

Cliff feels bad.

"I have other anxieties," he says. "It's just he brings everything to the surface."

"What other anxieties do you have? You are young, handsome, you seem in good health."

Cliff takes the compliments.

"I have this film here at the festival," he says. "And the film is very personal to me, so there's that stress, and then on top of that I didn't bring a copy with me, which I know is insane but I just didn't okay and so that's now a thing, because they don't have a copy of the film and everything is a mess. I've come all the way out here to show my film and I don't have my film to show. I'm angry about it, and I'm angry at a lot of people for it, but I guess what it boils down to is I'm angry at myself. There is no-one to blame but myself."

"You think this might be something to do with your mother?" says the pilot.

Cliff thinks.

The pilot seems to be in thought for a moment, and then he says, "Sounds like you could do with a break. You wanna see the Pyramids?"

Cliff isn't sure what to say. "What about the revolution?"

He gestures to the erupting violence on the bridge.

"We're good," says the pilot and he spirals his forefinger in the air.

The pilot dips his stick and the chopper veers off south at speed.

Cliff's hands reach up and he takes a firm grasp of the door frame. They move fast over rooftops, but the necropolis isn't far, and Cliff sees the Pyramids as if for the first time, coming up over houses, the greyness of Tahrir falling away to a golden light. These most famous of triangles look like scattered children's blocks, and the nose-broken chimera of the Sphinx to the south, its back to the princely edifices, is resplendent, more cat-like in attitude than it truthfully is in design.

Cliff holds his breath as the chopper swoops over the Pyramids, makes an uneven figure of eight between the peaks, and a line of tourists look up into the air in wonder.

"Wanna set down?" says the pilot.

The blades cause a minor sandstorm that upsets people, horses, and camels nearby.

Once down the pilot says, "Go ahead; go take a look around."

Cliff unpeels the headset from his scalp and climbs out of the chopper, keeping his head low until he's out of range of the blades, like they do in the movies.

He approaches the Pyramids slowly, thinking how silly of him it is to now notice their size, their famous hugeness, it is so stupid to be in awe of these things that are famous through time and space for their awe-inspiring stature. His feet sink deep into the light golden sand. The air is warm but thin, it feels good in his lungs, energising. He finds himself marching up to the central Pyramid of the three, the Great Pyramid, the tallest one, the widest one, its dishevelled, frayed exterior coming into focus sharply the closer he gets.

Out of the corner of his eye there is a figure, a guide, tall, in white robes and turban, grey specks of beard on his angular chin, standing next to an entrance, the entrance of a dark passage. He smiles at Cliff, bows at the waist. "Mr Robert," he says. Cliff bows back. He gets the sense there is something waiting for him in there, something alive, real. He feels – hears – a grunt or a slither. The darkness moves. A mass. A tentacle? Cliff feels calm, at home, and following the extended arm of the guide, he enters the darkness of the corridor, and the darkness, the absolute blackness of it, along with the coldness, is like submerging in water, and he can taste his mother's perfume, and it takes his breath away.

"…which is probably the kind of thing your mother would have said."

Lewis is still talking.

Cliff blinks. Rubs his eyes. He can still taste his mother's perfume.

"Why do you keep bringing up my mother?" Cliff says, straightening himself in the chair and wiping spittle from the corner of his mouth with the back of his hand.

He looks around the office. Everyone is busy, occupied; eyes, spectacles, reflecting the white squares of their monitor screens. Through them all he sees Rana is sitting at her desk but looking straight at him. Cliff half-smiles at her. She smiles back, but it's sad, sympathetic.

"I suppose there are several reasons why I've mentioned your mother twice now in conversation and I would argue both of them have been legitimate references pertinent to the topic of the moment, but as I said earlier there is something to be extracted from the intensity of human relationships that goes beyond the emotional and psychological impact they have on an individual and I think that is a place worth excavating for any script and in fact I think it's imperative perhaps even an obligation to mine those lands for our stories."

"I thought your script was about sea monsters in the desert." Cliff does not look at Lewis, does not turn away from Rana's gaze, as he interrupts Lewis successfully for what feels like the first time.

"On one level it is, and it is absolutely about monsters and about the excitement that monsters can bring to a story; I am, after all, only human... but I accept, and to a certain extent even encourage an interpretation of those monsters as metaphors but it is fundamentally important that they are monsters, ancient and colossal, and from the ice cold darkness of the deep, and I absolutely reject facile nonsense such as 'Jaws is not a film about a shark' which it quite clearly is..."

"I couldn't agree more. Of course it's about a fucking shark. It's like saying *Transformers* isn't about robots when HELLO there's fucking robots right up there on the fucking poster."

"Precisely." Cliff noticed the slightest of flinches from Lewis – was it the profanity?

"I suppose I am saying the metaphor does not negate the thrill of the obvious," Lewis says.

"Metaphors be damned," says Cliff.

The taste of his mother's perfume…

The sweet power of memory

…it's gone now.

"Metaphors aren't everything; it's true," says Lewis.

"Although," Cliff says, his grin dropping, "my movie doesn't have robots in it, or sharks, or sea monsters."

"And it's too late to put them in, I suppose?"

Cliff rubs the back of his neck with his hand and sighs deeply. His out-of-body experience, a daydream, nobody had even noticed he was out of it.

Perspectives, the pilot had said.

Cliff is across the room decanting from the water drum into a paper cone, one slug, refill, another slug, refill, watching the glugs of bubbles rise up through the water after each turn of the tap. Maybe the daydream had been good for him. Lewis seemed different. That exchange just now, it had been good. Perhaps Cliff hadn't noticed just how lonely he'd been all day.

He takes a deep breath and scrunches the cone up and tosses it into the waste-paper bin at the side of the drum and turns to return to his seat. He nearly tumbles straight over a line of people. They are three small women, big eyes in the centre of their headscarves, warm if unsure smiles aimed straight at him. They are the same height, the three of them, all about five feet tall. The one in the centre says, "Can we help?"

Cliff looks about himself, wondering if he's done something to illicit their rescue.

"I don't think so," he says, slowly, just in case he hasn't yet realised that he very much *does* need their help. "I was just thirsty."

He smiles.

They all smile back.

"Probably the food I had," Cliff says.

"Ah, Sammy took you for *koshari*," says the one to the left.

"He did." Cliff pats his breastplate and feigns a cough. "I found the chilli a bit strong."

"Yes, we heard about that."

They all laugh.

Cliff does too, although his is a little more strained.

"Sammy asked us to make sure you have everything you need," says the middle one. "I am Zariah," she says. "This is Lina," she points to the quiet one. "And this is Bahini."

"It is very nice to meet you, Mr Clifford," Bahini says.

"And you too," says Cliff. "And I'm very grateful for you offering to look after me, but there's nothing I need at the moment. But I also don't want to put any of you out of a job."

Their smiles do not drop.

"Oh, this is not our job," says Zariah.

"No," says Bahini.

Lina shakes her head.

All three of them retain their warm smiles.

"I am a senior production manager," says Zariah. "Bahini is our commissioning executive. And Lina is one of our development consultants."

"Oh," says Cliff, slightly embarrassed he had misread the room. "Forgive me for asking, but why are you three tasked with looking after me if you're in such senior positions?"

The three of them look at each other, as if the answer to the question is written on their faces. Zariah turns back to Cliff and says, "Because you are our guest."

They stand for a while by the water drum and talk. Cliff is not a big man – six foot on a good day when his shoulders aren't tight and his arches don't ache – but he towers over them. They talk for a while about the festival, how it works, what it does. "How long have you been working for Sammy?" Cliff asks, and they have varying answers but none of them have been there for more than two years. For Lina, the quiet one, it is her first few months, and she says to Cliff in a hushed voice that she is actually a student, studying women writers of Iran for her Masters. This seems weighty to Cliff. He doesn't know much about the Middle East, but like any good liberal he knows it's complicated and that the women of Iran don't have such a good time of it. He thinks of a photo he's seen a few times, of a liberal Iran, when the Shah ruled, and women drove cars and walked about the beach in swimwear. Bahini has a way about her as she talks about her ambitions in cinema. She is serious when she talks, that welcoming smile remaining on her mouth, but it's a little harder. She wants to eventually set up her own production company that only produces Arab women filmmakers. Zariah, the head of the triumvirate as they stand, has at her heart a passion for literature. She talks about Naguib Mahfouz, his dominant shadow cast over Egyptian letters, a great man, but now the future, the revolution, must bring with it new great writers. And they will be women, Zariah says. Cliff tries to keep up, the paper cone still crumpled in his hand.

"Do you know anything about these friends of Sammy we're supposed to be meeting with?" Cliff says.

The three look at each other, exchange some Arabic phrases.

"Interviews?" says Zariah. "You have interviews lined up with journalists."

"No, not that. Sammy wants me to meet some friends of his he says are trying to make a film about the revolution."

The three of them go cold, their smiles now drained of the warmth.

"We don't know anything about that, I'm afraid," says Bahini.

Cliff smiles, trying to be disarming, charming.

"Off the books, that one, eh?" he says.

The three inject a little more vigour into their smiles.

"Most likely," says Zariah.

Cliff isn't entirely sure they have understood his phrasing.

He thinks of a different angle.

"I have had an interesting morning," he says. "Sammy took us to Tahrir Square. Told us all about the uprising."

"He told you about his son?" says Zariah.

"A powerful story," Cliff says.

"Very sad," says Bahini. "Did you meet his nephew? Nabeel? He normally drives Sammy around."

"We had a driver, yes."

"That would be Nabeel, then," says Zariah. "Nobody else drives Sammy."

Strange Sammy wouldn't introduce him as his nephew.

Cliff looks across at Lewis slowly moving his finger around the screen of his tablet.

"He explained about the revolution," Cliff says. "How the government is trying to memorialise it as a 'disturbance'."

The three of them laugh edgily.

"No," says Bahini, her palm up to Cliff. "It was a revolution."

"Oh, I understand. I'm not saying I agree," says Cliff.

"A revolution," says Lina.

"Yes," says Cliff. "I completely agree."

"Don't be led to believing it was a disturbance," says Zariah.

"No, I'm not."

"It was no such thing, you understand."

"I'm just saying what Sammy said."

"You must understand."

"I do."

"Not a disturbance."

"A revolution."

Cliff looks at them all. They are very different now. They seem taller, older.

"*The* revolution," he says, in an attempt to emphasise his solidarity.

The shoulders of the three loosen up.

"Oh, no," says Zariah. "There have been others."

"And there will be more to come," Bahini says with a disarming nonchalance.

Cliff catches this. *More to come*.

"Do you mean imminent?" he says.

He isn't sure if they're feigning ignorance or whether he actually mumbled.

"Imminent?" says Bahini.

"I'm being introduced to some of Sammy's friends this afternoon, and I'm wondering what their involvement is in certain political movements."

"We wouldn't know anything about that," says Zariah. "Do you have enough water?"

"No, I'm good, thank you."

"May I just say," Bahini speaks up; "you may want to stick around the conference centre today if you can. Lots of opportunities here. And your film is not with us yet. We may need you."

"You have word about my movie?"

"Not as such," says Zariah.

Cliff looks past them to Rana at the far end of the office. She is on the phone. Chewing the end of a biro. Stern face.

"We *loved* your film," says Zariah.

"Loved it," says Bahini.

"Admired it greatly," says Lina, and she bows her head an inch.

The three of them are back to full warm energy, their smiles brightest, their eyes widest.

"It is an honour to have you here," says Zariah.

"Wait," says Cliff. "You've seen my movie?"

"Not *seen* it," says Zariah.

"But Rana has explained it in great detail," says Bahini.

"A beautiful story," says Lina.

"Told beautifully," says Zariah.

"We were very much looking forward to meeting you," says Bahini.

"Someone who can make such a work of art about their mother," says Zariah.

"We admired that most of all," says Lina, and she bows her head an inch.

"But you haven't *seen* it?"

Of course they haven't seen it. How could they have seen it?

The three look as if they are unsure what they could have said that was wrong. Cliff feels ingratitude written on his face. He tries to rescue himself.

"It is very gratifying to have such impassioned responses to my work," he says. "And I hope you enjoy it as much when you do actually see it."

Did that sound sour?

They look like it may have sounded at least a little sarcastic. So, he laughs. A light, chummy laugh. And they laugh along. Not so bad.

"And it's not about my mother," he says.

The smiles drop.

"Oh," says Bahini.

"But Rana explained the film quite thoroughly," says Zariah.

"It will be clearer when you see it."

"Your mother died while filming," Bahini says. "Rana explained that too. She called your film a perfect eulogy."

"She did?"

"I believe in the viewers' experience of cinema," he begins to say. "That every viewer brings with them to the theatre their set of emotions and experiences and even prejudices, and that can influence everything from images to the understanding of subtext. Perhaps Rana is giving her version of a film that is different to the one many others might see."

"No, Rana isn't like that," says Zariah with a warm smile. "She is very analytical. She has a Masters in critical theory and wrote her thesis on the social psychology of the influence of the matriarch on the male auteur."

"But we are excited to see it for ourselves this evening," says Zariah.

Ah, yes, this evening. Cliff looks once again across at Rana. She is still on the phone, still chewing the end of the biro, still looking stern. She hasn't moved. He wants to enquire, but she doesn't look ready to be disturbed.

"Do you know anything else about how the transfer is doing?" Cliff says to the three.

"Can I get you some tea?" says Zariah.

"Have *you* seen my film?" Cliff asks Lewis.

Lewis puts the L of his hand to his chin like a Regency poet awaiting his muse, or like the pensive emoji Cliff likes to send to Marie whenever she texts him a question he doesn't have time to answer.

"I've seen the poster," he says. "A girl on a swing."

"That doesn't answer my question. Have you seen the movie?"

Lewis nods. It's not evasive. If anything, it's uninterest.

"Actually," he says after a long moment, "Uncle Preston offered to give me a private viewing in his office, that private viewing suite he has out the back, have you seen it? He calls it a suite which I think is a bit grand, but he has those sorts of airs and graces, doesn't he? It's more of a small room with a sixty-inch TV in it and a row of upholstered chairs. I understand the need to build a persona, a brand, in this business."

"I know the room," says Cliff.

"Yes, so he invited me to the office and then told me about the trip and then showed me into 'the suite' and put the film on."

"And what did you think of it?" Cliff asks tentatively.

Lewis is not going to mince his words.

"What did I think of the movie?" Lewis says.

He's stalling.

Maybe he *is* going to mince his words.

"Yes; my movie."

Pause.

"What did you think of my movie?"

Lewis's straight back seems to straighten even further.

"Well, that day was put aside in my diary to work on my graphic novel."

"So, you *didn't* watch the movie? You declined?" Cliff says.

"I didn't decline. Uncle Preston wanted me to see it because of this trip."

Cliff is trying to work out what Lewis is saying.

"So, you sat through it. But you didn't watch it?" Cliff is leaning forward.

"That day was in my diary for work on my graphic novel."

Lewis takes his phone out of his pocket and waves it daintily at Cliff.

"Your graphic novel is on your phone?" Cliff says.

"I use an app called Tilemaster," Lewis says. "Some people find it a little basic, but I find it…"

"So, Preston put my film on for you and you sat there playing on your phone?"

"It's not playing on my phone. I'd put the day aside in my diary for work on my graphic novel…"

Cliff snaps out of his chair and when he reaches full stretch he lets out an almighty exhalation, just a puff, not a scream, but one loud enough for several people in the office to lift their eyes from their work. Rana is one of them. Zariah, Bahini, and Lina, too. Cliff leaves Lewis without a word and goes over to Rana's desk.

What has he gone over there for?

What's the plan?

Haven't got one really.

Just get away from Lewis for a second and take it from there.

Before Cliff says anything, if he was going to say anything at all, Rana says, "Good news. Your film is downloading." The pressure in his head eases. He looks at Rana, those long lashes and that strong jaw line; the rage that had been fizzing at his edges bubbles into something more resembling hope, and if he had been in a different country, and maybe if he had been a different person, he would have embraced her.

"Did you get hold of Preston?" Cliff says. Rana shakes her head regretfully and says simply, "Maggie."

Cliff looks over Rana's shoulder at the bar on her monitor screen.

It says: 9%. 9 HOURS to go.

"That is never accurate."

Sammy has joined them, is looking over Rana's other shoulder, and he says it almost with contempt: "It will say nine hours for six hours and then BANG it rushes through to the end and we're home and dry."

"Six hours?" says Cliff.

Sammy shrugs.

"More or less."

Cliff's first interview.

The first of several interviews over the next few days, Sammy tells him. The big national Egyptian newspapers, a couple of film magazines, and the Cairo television network, which has set up a temporary talk show studio complete with faux fireplace and conifers just across the mezzanine.

But this is to take place in Sammy's office, within full earshot of all his staff. Cliff is shown over to where the potted plant has been repositioned. A small round woman with a furrowed brow is waiting. Sammy introduces her, but Cliff isn't sure which is her name and which is the newspaper she's writing for, everything is said so quickly and much of it so unfamiliar to him. Cliff nods politely, shakes the woman's hand, who seems to take his reluctantly. Sammy leaves them to it. The woman's English is slow, she spends much time paused, searching for words, leaving Cliff sitting there in silence as she makes spirals in the air with her pen and stares off into the middle distance. She attempts a few ways to get to the first question.

How is he finding Cairo?

Cliff tries to answer.

He hasn't seen much of it yet, but he is very excited to be here.

He thinks of the CNN helicopter ride. Says, "I believe helicopter is the best way to see the Pyramids."

In good English the woman replies, "You could say that about almost anywhere."

"Yes," says Cliff. "Good point."

He laughs and tries to inject a little twinkle into his eye. It doesn't seem to work. It doesn't always.

"Have you travelled much?" she says.

These are not the in-depth questions Sammy promised. Icebreakers perhaps.

Cliff nods, puts on his best smile. Europe, the States, India, Japan. "I guess that counts as well-travelled."

"Even in this day and age," she says and looks down at the notepad open in her lap.

Her next question is about the film. She's not making any notes. Cliff wonders if she's understanding much of what he says, and he tries to talk slowly, but not so slowly as might be interpreted as insulting her intelligence. Is her English good or ropy? He moves between believing the two.

She looks bored.

"Tell me about your mother," she says, as if she's his therapist.

Cliff wipes his cheeks with the palm of his hand.

"The mother in the film is not my mother per se," Cliff says.

"Why not?"

He tries by postulating something about the nature of influence and the notions of creating fiction out of autobiographical impulses.

"So, she is *not* your mother?"

"No, she is *not* my mother, but I'm sure a part of my mother is in that character. It's inevitable," Cliff says.

"Was your mother as glamorous as the mother in the movie?"

Why does everybody want to talk about my mother all the time?

He decides to flip it.

"Do you think, from what you know of the film, that it will resonate with Egyptian audiences?" he asks her.

The woman thinks about it, but he can't be sure she has fully understood the question. And then, after much musing, she says, "No."

Cliff leans back in the chair, obscures himself from her with the potted plant.

"Your father is not in the film," she says to him.

"Neither is my mother."

He gently tugs at his collar as if a puff of steam will be released and cool him down, and he smiles at her again. This time he feels the glint come to his eye – that all important glint that has got him out of so many scrapes in the past, opened so many doors, even probably extracted that cheque from Preston's pocket. It has no effect on this woman, but at least he feels the return of the glint and he feels a bit more like himself. He needs to relax. He's been tense since Heathrow and blaming it all on Lewis won't wash. If Marie was here, she'd give him a dressing down. Focus, she'd say; show the woman a bit of respect.

Cliff smacks his lips together.

Why isn't his father in the movie?

Where *is* his father in all this? A quiet man. A small man. Narrow shoulders and when he smiled his entire face lifted up as if being operated by wires, his forehead would fold like a pug dog and the lines at the side of his eyes would crease like eagle's wings. Where *is* his old dad in all this?

Cliff exhales again, quieter than last time. He tickles his own rib cage, pushes it outward and trips his fingertips along it like it's a glockenspiel. A different tactic feels revelatory. A relief. He comes forward.

"Can I ask you another question?" he says to the journalist.

The woman shrugs.

"What do you think I'm doing here?" he says.

She turns her lip.

"I'm serious," he says. "Is it worth me being here?"

She looks at him with distaste; she's almost recoiling.

"I'm thinking this all over," he says. "Wondering if I may have just made a terrible mistake. That I may have spent all this time creating something nobody asked for. Do you think that's worth my time? Or do people not know what it is they want?"

She shrugs.

She makes a note in her book, the first one.

"What are you writing in there?"

"That you are rude," she says.

"Yes," Cliff says. He leans back. "I wasn't brought up that way," he says. "My dad wouldn't understand all this." He gestures to the conference centre they are in, the festival. "My mum: she knew glamour. To answer your question. I wouldn't say she had aspirations, but she had airs and graces. She wanted to be a star but was also happy with her lot in life. She would never have dreamt of getting up on stage or even going to drama school or learning an instrument. But she knew what it meant to be looked at. Stared at. And as she got old, she didn't get tacky, which most of her friends did. She stayed stylish. More Katherine Hepburn than Zsa Zsa Gabor. She would have understood all this, even though she never once took up one of my invitations to come to a party or a premier. Can't leave your father at home on his own, she'd say. Who'd cook his tea? He wouldn't understand all this. All the support they gave me over the years. For something they couldn't really engage with themselves. I suppose that's what being a parent is, isn't it?"

"Is your father still alive?" the woman says.

This catches Cliff. He is half submerged in a memory, bending decades into one second, the love – at arms-length always but never hidden, never muffled – of his mum and dad for him. The question caught him, and he isn't sure why he can't answer easily, quickly. He looks at the questioner, half-smiles, as if waking up.

"I'm not sure," he says.

Silence between them.

She holds the pen an inch above the paper.

"It's an honour to be here," Cliff eventually says. "It really is."

He offers his interviewer a smile, as relaxed and sincere as he can make it, and it seems to have some kind of effect on her. The woman's shoulders loosen up; although he hadn't taken her posture for tension, that must have been what it was, and when she does this her whole frame seems to open up and she loses some of that hardness, some of that anxiety. He can't quite remember what he just said. She asked something about his father. Did he just open up to her?

"Your film is very personal to you?" she says.

"Yes, yes, yes. Of course, all true works of art are personal. Even the commissioned piece of work has something of the artist in it. That's how it becomes great. That's the *only* way it becomes great. The Medicis may have paid Michelangelo to paint them at their best, but he gives the priest his own nose, and the cherub his mouth."

The woman looks confused.

"You have to bring your own soul to the work."

Cliff beats his chest – a gentle but firm rap.

The woman flinches.

"Sorry," he says. "I think maybe I'm tired. Jetlagged, perhaps."

The woman looks entirely unconvinced.

"Is your father not represented in your film because of his abandonment of you?" she says.

"Abandonment? He didn't abandon us."

"You said you don't know his whereabouts. I am sorry. I think my English is making for confusion."

But her English is good, sharp, clear at the most important points.

Cliff looks across the room at Lewis, still working away at his tablet pulled up just a few inches from the end of his nose.

"I had a dream," Cliff says, "that I was taken by helicopter to the Pyramids and I stepped out of it and a tall man, a guide, a local, an Egyptian, he showed me into the mouth a tunnel, and I went down it."

"And what did you see?"

Cliff ponders.

"What did I see? I didn't see anything. I just went down it."

The woman makes a note.

Cliff rises in his chair an inch to try and see what she's writing, but all he can see is Arabic. And he also sees sketches down the margins, small boxy drawings that he can't quite make out.

"Are those hieroglyphics?" he says.

She looks at him.

She looks at her page.

Then back up at Cliff.

"Of course not," she says. "Hieroglyphs are ancient. They are doodles. You have doodles in your country?"

Cliff lowers back down the inch he had risen.

"Yes, of course. Sorry. What are you writing now?"

"That you are stupid."

That could have been worse, Cliff thinks but stops himself from saying it out loud, unless it comes out as a mumble, because she looks back up at him sharply. Cliff, needing to look anywhere but at her, glances over his shoulder back toward Rana's desk. A small crowd has gathered there.

"Who are your influences as a director?" the woman says.

"One second," Cliff says.

He goes over to Rana's desk. Looks over her shoulder.

Thirteen hours.

The number on the download bar has changed from 9% to 10.

"Don't worry, Robert," Sammy says. "It will change in an instant. This is how things work here. I've seen it a thousand times."

"Why does it say thirteen hours?" Cliff says.

He realises he is pointing at the screen, his arm out straight and his hand somewhat limp at the end of it.

"It's supposed to go down, not up," he says.

"We will keep trying," Rana says.

Cliff looks at his watch, but his vision is blurry, his eyes are both dry and warm, dry *and* wet.

"Perhaps *I* can get hold of Preston," he says.

"We will still have to download it this end," says Rana.

"There must be somewhere in Cairo where the network can handle this kind of file?" says Cliff.

"There is very little wrong with the network," Rana says. "It is just a big file. Maggie didn't know how to compress it."

"You spoke to her?" Cliff says.

"Yes. This is her edit," says Rana.

That phrase again: *her edit*. What does that mean? What is *Maggie's* edit? Why has she even done one?

"But there must be a better way," Cliff pleads.

"Well, of course," says Sammy. "There must be."

But he offers no examples.

"The same thing happened to me in Nottingham, at a film festival there," says Lewis, at their side as if materialising from nowhere.

"What do you mean?" says Cliff.

"Bad internet," says Lewis.

Cliff already knows that not even the threat of strangulation would force a straight answer out of Lewis, so he instead looks again at his watch and tries to think of something else.

But he can't think of anything else.

Tears.

He can feel them start up in the back of the throat, that metallic ache, that's where they start. He's not a crier, doesn't consider himself one, but is also not a piece of stone, and he *has cried*. There is a distinction, for men, between those who *can* cry, and those who *cry at anything*. In this day and age that is an important distinction still. And Cliff wishes he could make that distinction here, to these strangers. But so far, the tears have not come, just the threat, and the threat has its own manifestations, the blushing of the cheeks, the reddening of the eyes. He has these, he can feel them come on as if the metallic ache to the back of the throat has spread there. And he can see the change in the faces of the people around him. Rana, Sammy, Zariah, Bahini, Lina – Lewis, even, for the first time, seems to have noticed a change in Cliff.

Rana stands.

Lewis is worried.

Sammy puts his hand on Cliff's shoulder and says, "Why don't you go and get some air? I will fix this. Go for a walk. Rana, will you take Robert and Lewis for a tour of the festival site? Perhaps get a nice refreshing cold drink." The big man looks at his wristwatch. "It is past noon. A cold beer, perhaps? In one hour, I will have this fixed, and then we go and meet those friends I promised to you."

Cliff has no idea how Sammy can fix it, but he's willing at this point to put the utmost faith in his warm and comforting tone.

Sammy looks at his watch again.

"But first," he says, "I have a meeting I cannot miss." And with his wrist still raised to his chest he walks off, out of the office.

What is there to do? *What a day, what a day.* He's not thinking of it right now, as it's all Cliff can do to stop himself hyperventilating, but somewhere in the deep recesses of his mind his mum is holding out her arms to him. But, oh dear, also in there is that scene from *The Exorcist* when Karras dreams of his own mother rising eerily from the subway in a hyperbright New York street. The breath. It's up there at the front. Perhaps the greatest evocation of a dream in all cinema. *Why did you leave me, Demi?* Not a good time to be thinking of that. It's coming up through him, Cliff's mum coming out of the ground, from between the paving slabs. She used to say to him, *What is your movie about, Robbie?* She was weak and sickly but her questions were always delivered firmly. Cliff would say it was just a little domestic tale of one man struggling to find his place in the world. A short story writer who has to make a living from writing for pornographic magazines. Cliff wouldn't mention that second part to his mother. One day this writer meets a girl. She comes to the house asking for donations to a refugee charity. He tells his mum it's a simple love story. He doesn't tell her that the girl, who is also shy and reclusive, is also a writer. They connect, and she visits the house regularly. The house where our protagonist lives with his mother. She visits and they share their work. There is an awkward triangle of man-woman-mother. The girl is quiet, polite, mousey. She's a better writer than our protagonist, it turns out. And she is on the verge of an artistic and creative breakthrough. Publishers circle. She is excited, but quiet about it. She tries to get her man a leg up, quietly, but the publishers aren't keen on his stuff. Truth is, everyone around him is a better writer than he is. Truth is, all he's good at – all he's good at in the world – and he's really great at it is writing pornography.". Cliff wouldn't tell his mum this part.

"Robert, you don't look well," says Rana with her hand on Cliff's shoulder. They haven't yet left the office, and Rana is thinking Cliff may need something before they venture for the tour that Sammy has encouraged. "Can I get you a glass of water? Some hot tea?"

The very idea of hot tea makes Cliff's chest tighten.

He looks at her, and for a second Rana is aglow, as if she is his designated saviour. Her headscarf, the way it frames her rounded face of flawless skin and dark eyes, it makes her angelic, an entity sent only to lift him to a higher plain. Marie might argue this is Cliff's view of most women. Most people.

"What can I get for you, Robert?"

"I need to phone home," he says.

Walking him to a private room, Rana is unconvincing when she says the screening will go ahead, and the prize will remain undisrupted, and there's nothing he has to worry about.

Lewis walks with them, a pace behind.

"I'm going to be making a private call," Cliff says.

Lewis continues to follow.

The room Cliff is shown to is uniformly off-white, almost stylised in that way. A single table in the centre with four chairs of white plastic and chrome. In the middle of the table is a four-way conference call hub. It looks space-age in this context, a small blot of ink in the infinite off-white of the universe.

"You can call here," Rana says, laying a soft hand on the hub. "Or you can link to the Wi-Fi and make a WhatsApp call if you prefer."

"And we can't use that signal to download my movie?"

Rana, with the softest of smiles, shakes her head slowly.

Of course not.

What, do you think these people are idiots?

Do you not think they would have thought of that already?

Lewis is loitering in the doorway, but when Rana leaves, she ushers him out with her.

Then, Cliff is alone.

He turns to the table, to the hub, exhausted. He is here, in this room, because for the first time he understands something Marie used to say to him at his darkest moments. She had a phrase, and it had stuck, contrary to his own beliefs, and to the fact his own behaviour in recent years suggested he had never really heard her when she said it. Marie had a way of compressing complex ideas into sentences, sentiments, that cut to the bone. She was a poet. A bloody poet. And now, in Cairo, in that conference centre, in that office, in that room, staring down at the stunted tentacles of that conference call hub, he could see her, leaning against the kitchen counter with her hands – big hands, she had big spindly hands – enveloping the radiating coffee mug, her work blouse yet to be tucked in, the morning light breaking through the kitchen blinds, and there would come this poetry, *her* poetry. She would say, "It's just a fucking film, Robbie."

When he calls her she's at the supermarket.

"I was listening to a podcast about the real lives of feminist icons," she says. "So, you realise interrupting that is a classic patriarchal move."

"I didn't know you were listening to it," Cliff says.

"Again, claiming ignorance… classic patriarchy. How could a woman be listening to a feminism podcast?"

"Surely the patriarchy believes that's *all* you listen to?" Cliff says.

"Yes, you're right. Thank you for correcting me on my own joke. When are you back?"

"You miss me?"

There is a chink here, a hairline of hope in Cliff's voice.

"No," Marie says. "I'm standing in the meat aisle and I'm wondering how many chicken breasts to buy. I forget if you're home for Paula and Brian coming over on Sunday. I could freeze one, I guess. When are you back?"

"Monday, I think." Cliff rubs his face. He hasn't quite thought about it. "But I'm not sure when my flight is, so it may be Tuesday by the time I get back home."

"Oooh, it's two-for-one on that butter you like."

Cliff smiles. He is sitting on one of the white plastic-and-chrome chairs, the phone to his ear, bent over, his head in his hand.

"The one with that Persian salt?" he says.

"Yeah. So, you can have some toast when you get back."

"I'll look forward to it."

There are tears, but they aren't pure sadness, pure frustration, pure anything. They are just an overspill of excessive emotion, he supposes. And the fact his head is bent over means he's getting quite snotty.

"I think I picked up some sniffles on the flight," he says, before she asks.

"Since the ban on smoking, air conditioning in planes is actually worse for you. Because of the recycled air. Isn't that ironic? Alanis Morrisette would've struggled to find a decent rhyme for recycled air giving you influenza and then fucks up your entire holiday."

There's a few seconds' silence. It sounds as if Marie is occupied.

"Have you heard from Dad?" Cliff says.

"You've barely been gone a day, Robbie," Marie says. "I'm going to see him this afternoon. I told you I'd text if there was any change. And obviously I'll call if he croaks."

Cliff laughs, a coughed exhalation pleased with its own authenticity.

"Yes, a call would be good if he dies," he says.

"You'll have to wait for off-peak, though," Marie says. "I'm not fucking made of money."

"I wouldn't want to put you under any financial strain," Cliff says.

"To be honest, I wasn't really expecting you to call. You wouldn't normally; not for a trip that's only a few days long. There's obviously something up. What is it?"

Cliff takes a deep breath. He's still curled over in the seat.

"Everything's fine," he says.

"Oh dear," Marie says.

"Why 'Oh dear'?"

"We're back to *everything's fine*. You said that to me every other day during filming, and every day during the edit. So, something *is* wrong. Have they buggered up the film? Did they invite the wrong Robert Clifford? Have you gone to the wrong Cairo?"

"Everything's fine."

A sigh. Her, and then him.

The thing he hasn't said to Marie is that his obsession with the film had been born out of fear. Fear of being no-one. Fear of being just another guy. Fear of not fulfilling some unwritten dedication to the marvel of life, that we must strive to do something remarkable otherwise it's all been a waste of the most heinous nature. The fact that what truly separates man from the animals is that man believes you have to make your life *mean* something. *Create* something meaningful. But worse than this, he has known for a long time what a crock of shit that is. It's a crock of shit that life is special, or precious, or divine. The truth is, the further he got into making his film, the harder it was to abandon it. That was all. He'd spent too long talking about it, spent too long dismissing everything else. He didn't want to be the butt of a joke; he didn't want to feel embarrassed. He didn't want to be the man who failed. And so that's why he missed the death of his mother. He wasn't even sure what day it had happened, when it came down to it.

"I love you," Marie says.

The phone goes dead. He also didn't tell her that Sammy may — *or may not* — have offered to fix the prize in his favour in order to lure Preston into financing a documentary about a gang of Arab revolutionaries. He didn't tell her that.

No fucking way. He didn't tell her that.

Cliff has come out of the off-white room, revivified, feeling like some focus has come to him, and just as he strides back into the office, he sees two new figures, standing by the potted plant, talking to Sammy. *No fucking way.* What are they doing here?

He feels the positivity drain out of him like he has a crack in his foot.

Is there any way he could be mistaken?

No. It's them.

First, there's Deb Dallow. Unmistakable, even in a room that pays tribute to her height and porcelain paleness. She is statuesque, propped up by a silver cane – that's new – her elegant clothes shapeless, a complex system of folded robes and silks and lace; she doesn't walk into a room, she unfurls into it. She has a voice straight out of Tennessee Williams, one that goes out of her like a log flume. She talks about her hometown of Biloxi as if it's simultaneously Mordor and Graceland, and she does it with a tilted head, her face leaning back as if her nose and lips were in danger of sliding off if she straightened up. Cliff has always recognised her charms: a thoughtful face, pointed features, high cheeks, narrow eyes; and in the ten years or so they have been crossing paths she seems to have reached her correct age, that age when all the eccentricities, the myths and stories, the difficulties, when they have all come together to find a distinct coherence. Professionally, there is a seductive rationale to all this. She is a producer, although Cliff can't remember the last time he saw her name on a credit. Rumour has it she works much deeper behind the scenes nowadays. Whatever that means. Every time he meets her, she is working for some different organisation that he has never heard of. Deb Dallow has taught Cliff many lessons over the years. Most notably, that people can be talked into anything. If she has a philosophy, that is most likely it.

Second, is the man stood to Deb's left. Lean, expressionless, in a cheap olive suit that hangs off him like it's been draped over a tree stump while the owner goes skinny-dipping: the dark-eyed figure of Howard Phillips. He is creepy. He lingers, loiters. Cliff had honestly thought Howard was dead. Had somebody told him that? He had memories of someone somewhere sometime saying something like, "Howard Phillips is dead?". Or did somebody finally just *tell* him Howard was dead? But he looks very much medically alive in this office. The thing that makes him stand out in this instance is the thing he has on his head, a garment that sits there like a pimple, one that speaks without subtlety of both smallness and loudness all at once. Howard Phillips is wearing a MAGA cap. It sits there, unsuited as any hat would be to this gormless head; a head propped on his knotty shoulders like a castle turret made of repurposed gravestones. The cap, pulsating red as if something that should be operating inside his body is now exposed on the outside. Cliff has never before noticed quite what a glorious metaphor the MAGA cap actually is. The fact it is on the head of Howard Phillips is not quite the shock it should be. Howard is an American filmmaker, and one who made some ripples with films in the mid-noughties when he was starting out. A film about a woman obsessed with masturbating who eventually destroys an entire town. Cliff can never remember what it's called, but in his head it's called *Marla: A Fistful of Dynamite*. Howard also directed a film about angels called *Ingrate* which earned him a walkout at Cannes (although some say it was just because it was the lunchtime showing and the flyer had printed the run time as ninety minutes rather than the actual 490 minutes). He also made a film about a wheelchair-bound serial killer called *The Devil has Two Wheels*. In the last decade, as Howard's financiers began to shrink away from movies that had no tract with the sensitivities of a growing liberal American sensibility, Howard began to make documentaries. It was these that won him awards, armfuls of them, from organisations called things like The Association of Moving Pictures for Jesus, and *RedCarpetBomb Magazine*; he won the New Republic Stars of the Future Award in 2015 for a six-hour documentary entitled *Truth or Dare: The Crushing of the American Left*. Cliff still hasn't seen that one.

"Deb, I had no idea I'd be bumping into you here," Cliff says.

Deb Dallow is very good at pretending she hasn't seen you coming, even though she made fleeting eye-contact with Cliff the moment he stepped into the office.

"I am here meeting with Sammy. Introducing Howard to Sammy. This will be like when DeMille met Goldwyn, you can quote me on that."

"Are you still producing?" says Cliff.

"I am Head of Development at the Cinematic Council for Europe."

"Isn't it called the European Film Council?"

"No, I don't work for them anymore. I am very happy now in

Nicosia."

"Nicosia? Not Brussels?"

Deb waves her hand dismissively and leans heavily onto her cane.

"The Cypriot climate is good for my lungs," she says, and takes a few deep breaths.

Cliff almost signed up to make a feature film in Cyprus several years ago. An adaptation of a little-known novel about a mad artist who wants to paint dreams. Something like that. Cliff was doing nothing at the time, and it was only at the last moment he decided not to put his signature on the contract after rudimentary research revealed the finance was largely traceable to dodgy Russian enterprises who were based on the island. It wasn't a very sophisticated scam. Money laundering, was how Marie phrased it.

Lewis is at Cliff's side, as if from nowhere.

Cliff, recognising the awkward silence, turns to him.

"This is Lewis Proudfoot," he says. "A young filmmaker who's at his first Cairo festival."

"Isn't this *your* first, Robert?" says Deb with a sly look in her eye.

"It is." Cliff quickly changes tack. "I am here in competition."

"What is the competition for?" Howard speaks in a grating drawl.

"Of course, you two already know each other," Deb says.

Sammy is trying to explain amongst the stilted introductions that Deb and Howard will be joining them for dinner that evening, after the screening of Cliff's film.

"Yes, yes; and how is that thing coming along?" says Cliff to Sammy, almost under his breath.

"Problems?" says Deb.

"None at all," says Cliff.

"Trouble downloading the movie," says Lewis; his first vocal contribution to proceedings.

"Downloading?" says Deb, turning her tiled face to Cliff. She is suppressing a smile.

"Yes, yes, there was a bit of a mix up," says Cliff. "One that is being resolved as we speak; isn't that right, Sammy?"

Sammy shrugs, which doesn't help any, and then he says, "I'll go and check on it." He moves off with the air of a man grateful for the excuse to move off.

"This must be stressful for you?" says Deb.

Cliff offers a short sharp turn of the corners of his mouth that may in other circles have been regarded as a smile.

"What brings you here, Howard?" Cliff says instead. "I heard you were… retired."

"Huh, well, in some ways that is true, for it is necessary to be dead in order to be reborn," Howard says.

He sounds different.

"Is that a new accent you have there, Howard?" Cliff says. "Are you sounding a bit *southern*? Aren't you from Vermont?"

"It's true I have picked up a bit of what one might term a *twang* when embedded in the communities of my latest project."

"And what project is that?" says Cliff.

"I have just finished a documentary about the hip-hop group, Horn of Plenty. Have you heard of them, Robert? Perhaps a bit too cutting edge for you?"

Cliff has not heard of them.

But Lewis has.

"Aren't they the white supremacist hip-hop group? They purport to be reclaiming black music for the white man. They have connections to the Ku Klux Klan."

"That has been proven to be untrue," Howard says.

"Their first album was called *In the Grasp of the Grand Wizard*," says Lewis.

Howard's deathless gaze flutters and he looks at Lewis for the first time. Lewis has his lips now delicately wrapped around a straw that descends into some neon-blue ice slush drink.

"Where did you get that?" Cliff says.

"One of those three nice women got it for me. They could probably get you one."

"Did you just ask?"

"They offered."

Cliff thinks.

"I might get one," he says, biting his bottom lip, glancing over to where Zariah, Bahini, and Lina's desks are.

"I can ask," Lewis says.

"Really?"

Lewis slurps.

"Sure."

And he walks over to them with that straight-backed glide of his.

Sammy returns.

"Well? Any news?" says Cliff.

"I cannot bear the tension," Deb says.

Sammy forces a reassuring smile.

"It will be fine," he says.

"It will?" says Cliff. "You want to run any more details by me?"

The forced smile again.

"No," says Sammy. And he raises his arms. "Now, we go to the *hammam*!"

"The what?" says Cliff.

Everybody else seems to understand what Sammy's talking about. Something had been decided in Cliff's absence. Sammy puts his arm around Cliff and positions his mouth so close to his ear Cliff can feel the bristles of Sammy's stubble on his lobe.

"The first step in your next masterpiece," Sammy says.

In the back of the 4x4, Cliff is facing Howard Phillips, whose deathless eyes glare across at him from under the peak of his MAGA cap; his long, curved jaw undulating beneath his mouth like a wheel of cheese. Deb Dallow is locked in with Lewis.

Lewis the Trap.

Lewis the Weapon.

Lewis the Fearless.

Cliff has his blue slush drink. The efficiency was impressive. The sugar content equally so.

Cliff leans into Howard and adopts a hushed tone.

"You know every director who has ever worked with Deb has met with a mysterious end," Cliff says.

Howard glances over to Deb, still at this stage affecting the look of an interested party as Lewis walks her step-by-step through his script.

"I don't know what game you're trying to play," Howard says, straightening himself in his seat and looking out the window. His voice still has that southern twang, but it's more refined now, more plantation owner than trailer park inhabitant. "And your tongue is blue," he says.

Cliff smacks his lips together, as if that would return his tongue to its natural colour.

"No games. Just wondered if you knew what her nickname is?" Cliff says.

"Let me guess," Howard says, his eyes fixed on the passing roadside. "Is it Fade to Black?"

That's good.

Cliff sits back in his seat.

Rolls his blue tongue around in his mouth.

The air conditioning in the car has given everything that chilled veneer. Cliff is back-to-back with Sammy who is on the phone in the passenger seat. The driver is the same young man as earlier. Cliff turns and taps him on the shoulder.

"Sammy didn't tell me you were his nephew," Cliff says.

The man, who Cliff can now see is scandalously handsome with that sturdy nose and jawline, looks into Cliff's eyes, smiles unsurely and shrugs. He knows no English.

Cliff turns back to his view of Howard Phillips, rigid, distant.

"Where are we going?" Cliff says.

"The *hammam*," Howard says.

"What is the *hammam*? And why are we going there?"

Howard seems put out by the questions, and he just manages to stop his eyes at half roll.

"We're going to meet Sammy's friends," he says.

Cliff is still thrown by Howard's new southern twang, but he gets over it with a figurative shake of the head.

"You're coming to meet the revolutionaries?"

This seems to get Howard's attention.

"They weren't described to us in quite those terms," he says.

"Maybe we're meeting different people," says Cliff.

"Maybe," says Howard.

Deb is flagging, and when she does so it comes out in her face without edit. It's as if she's gasping for air. Lewis, of course, cannot read it at all, and he ploughs on, furrowing her sanity and plopping in his seeds of attrition along the grooves he makes. Cliff catches random words that form an impression not at all random: *ancient ones*, *tentacular*, *reckoning*, *Nietzsche*, *cheese sandwich*, something that sounds like *orange blossom*. Lewis is giving her the full works. Deb is close to becoming a mass of ticks and jerks, and she is saying, "This can be done; of course, it can be done."

Sammy is off the phone.

"Sammy, are we *all* going to meet with your friends?"

"Indeed, we are, Robert. I cannot wait for you to meet them."

Cliff shuffles and twists so that he can whisper, or at least talk in a lower, more private tone, into Sammy's ear.

"But I thought this was just a meeting for me and Lewis?"

Sammy twists back and his face and Cliff's face are now strangely close.

"I did not say that," he says.

"But why are Howard and Deb coming too?"

"They have ideas just like you do, Robert."

"But I don't have ideas. I didn't even want to come."

"So, what's the problem?"

"I think if you're kidnapping us, the least you could do is pay me the courtesy of kidnapping just me. Or just me and Lewis."

Sammy's face softens.

"Robert, are you okay? I must know you are okay."

"Of course I'm okay. I'm just trying to explain the whole thing. To myself."

"Are these friends of yours movie producers?" Cliff says.

Suddenly, somehow, Lewis is sitting next to Cliff and very much a part of this conversation. Cliff looks over Lewis's shoulder at Deb who appears to be gasping for air in the corner of the 4x4.

"They are producers," Lewis says.

"They are producers in the sense that they will be the ones who hire you, if you see eye to eye, to create this new picture," Sammy says.

Cliff notes that Sammy has raised his voice, and is addressing everyone in the 4x4 now, even changing his vernacular to *pictures* for the American in the room.

Cliff looks at everyone in turn, but saves his unhappiest glare for Sammy, on whom his final look rests.

"Are we pitching for work?" Cliff says. "Are you pitting us against each other?"

"I am giving my friends options, and you can see who fits," Sammy says.

The car pulls to a stop. Out of the corner of his eye, out on the pavement, Cliff sees Rana is standing in a doorway. He immediately feels the heat rise up on the back of his neck.

"Why is Rana here?" he says. "Why isn't she working on getting my movie transferred?"

"Our meeting is in a *hammam*," says Sammy. "Women cannot enter. At least not at this time of day. Rana is here to keep Deb company."

Cliff rubs the nape of his neck vigorously. He's feeling so many contradictory feelings about this meeting right now that he is having trouble expressing any of them.

Why are we having the meeting here if women cannot attend?

Why are we having a meeting with Howard and Deb present?

Why are we meeting with enemies of the state?

Why are we meeting?

That's the important one.

Why are we meeting?

Rana can answer. She seems like someone who isn't playing any games.

Cliff gets out of the car in a hurry, as if he feels the need to get to Rana before anybody else does. She smiles at him, as if she is a concierge bracing for a complaint.

"What are you doing here?" Cliff says, trying to sound as friendly as possible.

"We go for dinner after your meeting," she says. "Just across the way."

She gestures with an open palm across the street of zipping scooters and chugging tuk tuks.

Cliff barely looks.

"But, *my film?*"

It has only just occurred to him that Rana might be on this street because the film has been downloaded and it is all there waiting to screen. It is like a pin prick in his side, an acupuncture of hope. He feels his mouth open ajar in expectation, a smile coming to its corners.

"Your film is downloading," Rana says.

Cliff's smile drops. That pin is a sword.

"Shouldn't you be there making sure it all goes through? Last time I looked we seemed to have been getting further away from the point of celebration, not closer to it. Sorry, I don't mean to raise my voice."

"Robert, Robert, have some faith," Sammy says, patting him on the shoulder. "Rana is here to keep Deb company while we go and meet our friends. Then we will join them at Princes when we are done. You must try the *molokhia* when we get there. It is the best in Cairo."

"I don't know what that is," Cliff says. His brain is burning, and by the time this line comes out of his mouth it is like a steam signal of defeat.

Sammy begins to explain the intricate process of the *molokhia* soup, how it is prepared and poured at the dining table. Princes, the eatery across the street, is famous for it, he says.

"My film, Sammy. Why does nobody seem quite as concerned that my film won't be ready to show at 8pm tonight as I am? That can't be just faith, surely? Either nobody cares, or you all know something I don't know. So, which is it?"

Quite a long pause, in which Cliff looks at all of his fellow travellers – Lewis, Sammy, Howard, Deb, and Rana, and nobody replies to him in any haste.

"I have to say, Robert," says Sammy after a while, "I don't think any of us know anything you yourself don't know."

Sammy puts his arm around Cliff's shoulder and walks him a few yards away from the others.

"You are stressed, Robert," he says, "and I don't want that. How can I assure you everything is going to be just fine? How can I make things better?"

"Get the film sorted," says Cliff.

"I don't want anything to be lost in translation."

"Well, no, neither do I."

Sammy seems serious.

"I hope this meeting goes well," Sammy says. "And then perhaps there is not so much pressure on this film downloading."

"Pressure for what?" Cliff is pushing. "I spent years on this film, Sammy. It *has* to show."

"But the prize," says Sammy. "That's what gets you on to the next project. You said so yourself."

"Yes… but…"

Sammy puts his hand on Cliff's shoulder.

"What happens next is all that matters."

They have moved into the reception area of the *hammam*, and Sammy is explaining to the attendant on the desk that he has not booked an appointment but that they are all here to meet with someone who has. Cliff, whose mind for the last ten minutes or so has been dancing, rolling, careering, through the mesh of ideas he has been confronted with, finds in the glances of Rana a calmness, and a necessary calmness at that.

Rana steps across to Cliff.

"You should not worry," she says.

"I'm not worried," Cliff says.

"You look worried," Rana says.

"I'm not."

"There is nothing to be concerned about. These friends of my father, they are thinkers." She gently taps her temple with her forefinger. "They are not revolutionaries." She is speaking in a half-whisper as Sammy's voice grows louder in frustration at the attendant.

"They're not revolutionaries?" says Cliff.

"Not in the way you think," says Rana.

"What is the way I think?"

Rana makes a pistol with her fingers and fires them into the air making little shot noises with her pursed lips.

"I know my father can be overpowering," she whispers on. "He only understands getting his own way. Do this for him, meet with them, and then we can get back to the festival."

Cliff thinks for a second. He isn't sure he should say what it is he is about to say. No, that's not true; he knows he should not say it, but is going to anyway.

"Rana… your father said if I agree to take this film on for his friends he can fix the prize so I win. He thinks that will guarantee investment. He even suggested the film wouldn't need to be shown in order to win."

Rana's face is difficult to read at first.

"Do you think you might have misunderstood?"

A possibility.

"I want my film to be shown. I put my soul into it. I am dedicated to it."

Rana is thinking again.

"We do not cheat," she says finally.

He's offended her.

He looks across at Sammy, whose remonstrations with the attendant seem to be making progress. A man who gets what he wants no matter how much he has to push.

"You should go where your heart takes you," Rana says, and it feels like a statement both filled with ancient wisdom and a dead bat to end their conversation.

Cliff stands alone now. Rana has moved away. He thinks about his fear in the hotel room that morning. He thinks about Lewis. He thinks about the critic on the mezzanine, about his film being absent; the interview, his mother, his father, Marie at home. He thinks of Zariah, Bahini, and Lina, a trio of beautiful humans stooping to cater to him. Stooping. He thinks about what he is doing here. He used to look on things like this, these accolades, these events, and long for the keys to the castle. But what does any of it mean? Did Sammy offer to fix the prize for him? Or did he assume something? What does it mean if he did? Cliff feels a rivulet of sweat run down his spine. It's as if he's spent seven years inside his own head, and now he's stepping out into the light like a hermit from his cave. All of these people deserve more from him.

They all deserve more.

He thinks of Deb Dallow, sitting outside now on a roadside bench smoking her long thin Russian cigarettes, her head and arms growing like shoots out of the uncompromising folds of her robes. She is beautiful. Strong. She gets things done. And she looks lonely out there.

He thinks of Howard Phillips, a man sold to the idea of being forever discussed. But is that it? What does he get out of all this?

And then he thinks of Lewis once more, standing over by the old Coca Cola vending machine, looking it up and down as if it's an item of wonder.

Cliff steps over to him.

"If this works out," Cliff says, "we could work on this film together."

Lewis looks at Cliff.

He is thinking.

"*My* film?" Lewis says.

"No," says Cliff. "The film these guys want making."

Lewis looks blankly, as if he hasn't understood what Cliff just said.

"I'm not making anybody else's film," he says. "I'm making my own."

"But we're not here about your film. We're here about theirs."

Again, blank.

"I'm here about mine," Lewis says. "Do you have any money? I'd like a coke."

The remonstrations have stopped. The attendant has disappeared into the darkness of the corridor to fetch something or check something and get some answers. Sammy is texting on his phone. Rana has gone out to check on Deb. Lewis is drinking his coke.

"You might want to take that off," Cliff whispers to Howard.

"What?" says Howard.

"These men won't be admirers of your man," Cliff says, pointing to the cap on Howard's head with his eyes.

Howard lifts his large hand up to the cap and runs his hand across the printed text, like braille, as if he'd forgotten it was up there.

"This hat shows them I take my politics very seriously," he says.

No, it doesn't.

Cliff realises, if he wants this gig it's there for the taking.

Marie had said to take it. He hadn't gone into detail. He didn't want to worry her with talk of revolutionaries. Just said there were some guys he was meeting about a documentary project. On the phone, when she was shopping and probably only half-listening, she had said to take it. But what had her tone been? At the time it felt determined, supportive, but now Cliff thinks back on it, he wonders if it wasn't defeated, dismissive, a casual, protected, do-what-the-fuck-you-like. He listens back on it in his head. Do what the fuck you like. Marie's voice. She'd said that before, hadn't she?

Many times.

But, I mean, more recently, more pointedly.

Just before he left for the airport.

That's why she was surprised to get his call. There was a moment where Marie had hope, as the ringtone whizzed, as Cliff's name flashed up, that picture of him half distracted waving the camera away on a picnic bench overlooking the sea in West Wales. Hope he was going to apologise, admit his error, the broken promises. He shouldn't have come here. He had promised things would be different after the film was done. She had said, "A film can win a prize without you being there. Just like your father can die without waiting for you. Both are true, but only one matters." Just this one more thing. Get the prize and it all means it was worth it.

Sammy has won his argument, it seems. The attendant is back to tell them they can go deeper into the *hammam*.

"Go on, go on," Sammy says.

Suddenly, Cliff feels a weight in his gut. What is he letting himself in for?

What will it be like making a film for these revolutionaries? Will he be pushing a cameraman down a corridor like this one, trying to direct in the bad Arabic he's picked up from the hotel in the days spent prepping for some cataclysmic set-piece. What will they *need*? Do these revolutionaries have a relationship with notions of history? Is Cliff to evaluate this now, quickly, with a towel around his waist, wiping sweat out of his eyes. What if they want to blow up the Pyramids? That would be quite a statement and it has a definite cinematic attraction to it.

My God.

What if they want me to film them blowing up the fucking Pyramids?

Cliff is walking, his feet feel heavy, he is walking through the lobby with its garish throws, red-iron benches, its bird cages, the 80s Coca Cola machine, the mural of the Hanging Gardens of Babylon that adorns the wall behind the reception counter and one big glistening eye and is that a giant tentacle reaching over the balustrade of the palace? No, Cliff double-takes; just a branch, part of the hanging garden.

"Come, come," calls Sammy. "To the *hararah*."

They walk; Sammy, followed by Howard, followed by Cliff, followed by Lewis.

Cliff looks at everyone, tries to gauge their thoughts on this. Howard has nothing to offer, that gaunt hanging visage like a shelf of sandstone falling into the sea. Lewis, however, does something remarkable; he offers Cliff what can only be interpreted as a supportive smile, his eyes glisten and grow big, and his mouth turns from a wide thin slit into a curved progress chart. He even has a spring in his step. And then Cliff sees it. Lewis has that script in his hand.

"Why do you have that out?" Cliff says.

Lewis looks down at the wad of paper in his hand.

"This?" he says. "This is my script."

They continue down the corridor, between garish wall-hangings, Cliff's forward motion growing heavier in the thick air.

"I know *what* it is," Cliff says. "*Why* are you holding it?"

"To talk to the producers."

It's all so hopeless. Why is he here? Why are any of them there? God, it's so hot in here. The corridor is narrowing, lowering, rising, Sammy ahead of them filling the extremities with his frame, tall lumbering Howard in his MAGA cap dipping his head further and further as they go along, the deep reds and burned umber of the wall-hangings getting darker, steam coming toward them now, and Cliff's linen shirt and linen trousers are becoming saturated, and he looks back at Lewis who has forsaken his new chirpier demeanour and is now beginning to feel the heat, feel the pain, feel the suffocating steam soaking the bedding of his lungs. Cliff looks ahead, toward the end of this tunnel, to the mouth of the water room, the *hararah*, the baths. The steam. *God, it's so hot in here. Am I going to bloody pass out?* There is a dim light, the glistening reflection of fresh water, and Cliff can almost feel it on his skin. He can hear voices, and even this sound cools him down a little, the idea that people are there alive and conversing at the end of this tunnel of hell. But then he sees something move beyond the doorway to the *hararah*, something slithering, long and tentacular. And then he sees a man poking his head around the door. Is that the guide from his dream of the Pyramids? The steam rises thicker and it has an aroma. It's in Cliff's throat. God, it's his mother's perfume.

A phone.

Cliff's phone.

Ringing.

He scrambles in his pocket.

It's Marie.

He turns, pushes past Lewis, Sammy calling back after him.

Out in the street, in the world, Cliff takes the call, gasping for breath in the relative cool of the street breeze. He is about to call out, Marie what's wrong, is it Dad is he dead I'll be right home next flight I'll be there and I'll never leave again and this time I mean it. But nothing comes out.

Silence.

There are two ways this can end.

Many more than two ways, in fact, but for the sake of coherence and fidelity, you have two options.

Other options include Cliff going back into the *hammam* and meeting the revolutionaries, and they get on and Cliff finds they are actually just a bunch of college kids who want to see some change in their country after the promises of the revolution were undermined and diluted until officially forgotten. The college kids are horrified by Howard's MAGA cap, and even more horrified by his personality, and so enter discussions with Cliff to make a documentary about their movement which tracks the history of it in the context of the Arab Spring, and they even promise Cliff full creative control because sculpting the message is what those they criticise would do. They like Lewis, but he keeps banging on about Manga and Lovecraft and they feel he isn't quite right for this project, but they'd be happy if Cliff took him on as an assistant or something. Cliff isn't sure, but they all have a bit of a laugh about it and it all ends with Cliff grabbing Lewis in a headlock and ruffling his hair with his knuckles.

That's not one of the two, though.

Another not of the two, is that the silence Cliff hears down the line is slowly subsumed by the crackles and slithers of the ancient forgotten language of Cthulu and Cliff is turned into a zombie slave.

Tempting, but not quite right for this.

The first real option is one that reluctantly makes itself obvious at this stage, one that brings many themes together, and is one that suggests defeat for the protagonist but with the hope he can be redeemed off camera at a later date. This option goes something like this.

Silence.

And then Marie's voice.

"Cliff?"

Cliff is unable to say whatever it is he wants to say. Whatever that is.

He says nothing, but Marie feels he is there, feels she understands his silence, that he has seen hope in the silence, hope despite the odds, despite the obviousness, hope beyond hope. Marie said she would only call for one reason and one reason only.

"Your dad died," she says. "I arrived at the home this afternoon and they said they had been trying to call you and were just about to call me. It happened a few hours ago."

Silence.

Cliff looks back at the *hammam* and sees Lewis is there in the doorway staring back at him. The road is busy, but not loud, and Lewis offers Cliff a little smile.

Cliff has tears, but he is not sobbing, and his nose is snotty, but he's not falling apart. He says to Marie, "I'll be back, of course. First flight tomorrow. Dad would have wanted me to be here for the screening."

Reservation in Marie's response, like the glass surface of a calm lake. "Of course," she says. "Let me know what time you land. I'll pick you up from the airport. Good luck with the screening."

"Thanks."

"Love you."

"Love you, too."

That is the first of the two options, of the two on offer. And it is less of an ending than just the place where the story stops. The stopping point. You imagine the rest of their lives in your own time, with your own needs guiding it.

And then there is the second of the two options.

In the silence is hope. It's touch-and-go for a second. Cliff understands how, given the two options, the worst is always how it trends.

Silence.

"Cliff," says Marie. "Your dad wants to talk to you."

His father's voice, clear, if a little weak and rugged.

"Just wanted to wish you luck."

Cliff feels the choke in the back of his throat.

"Thanks, Dad. I'll be home on Tuesday – I *think* – and if I've won a little statue I'll bring it straight to you. I'm sorry I'm not there now."

"Don't be daft, Rob. You are doing exciting things. I spent forty years with my bare hands building houses and there you are in bloody Egypt with a film you made about your mother. She'd be so proud of you, son."

It's not *about* my mum.

Marie's voice. "I hope that gives you a bit of a boost, Robbie; you sounded quite down on the phone earlier."

"You know, I'd almost forgotten our fight," Cliff says. "Before I left. It's been otherworldly here. Time compressed but also stretched."

"It wasn't really much of a fight," Marie says. "I was just a bit pissed off to be left holding the bed pan yet again. After you promised it wouldn't be like it was with your mum."

"Sometimes I don't see the bigger picture."

"Let's not open this up now, eh?" Marie says. "It doesn't make you any more noble just because you realise finally what a dick you've been."

"So, you get the final word at this juncture?"

"I absolutely do, while I'm sitting here with your dying dad…" – he hears her smile at his dad as she says it – "…and you're sunning it up in Cairo. Yes, I absolutely do."

"That seems fair."

"Go and enjoy the accolades, your dad will be fine. If there's any change I'll call; otherwise, see you Tuesday."

"Okay."

"Oh, and Robbie," Marie says.

"Yes?"

"Seven years, and I've never once offered an opinion on this: but your film is about your mum. Get on board with that and it'll do a lot better."

That is the second of the two options.

If you've decided on running with option two, the more hopeful avenue of pursuit, then there are still things that need tying up. You can stop a story with a death, particularly if it's a death that implies a forced redemption of a defeated character, as does the death in Ending Option One. But Ending Option Two has much still to be resolved. So here we go...

Rana is at Cliff's side.

Lewis remains in the doorway across the street, trying with strange jerks of his shoulders to find a gap in the traffic between them so he can cross to the restaurant.

"Are you okay, Robert?" says Rana.

"My father," he says holding up the phone. "Wanted to wish me luck for the screening tonight."

Rana smiles.

"So, he is okay?"

"For now." Rana knew Cliff's father is ill? "How did you know?"

"We were told you might not be coming."

"Who told you that?"

"Preston," Rana says. "He said your father was very sick, and that you would have to stay at home to look after him. And then he said you were determined to come, and that he would arrange for someone to travel with you, to look after you, to make sure you had someone at your side, for support, for company."

They both look across the street at Lewis Proudfoot, still trying to get himself across the street. Some gaps in the traffic last nearly ten seconds, but this is still not enough for him. They watch him a while, dicing with death.

"Preston sent Lewis to look after *me*?" Cliff says.

"Yes," says Rana.

"He told me I was supposed to be looking after *him*."

Cliff feels nauseous but it passes in a second and he breaks into a wry smile.

Sammy parts the traffic, it seems to stop or slow down for him and he marches across, palms held up, with Lewis in his wake.

"I have had a call," Sammy says. "About your movie. We need to get back to the office."

"Where is Howard?" says Cliff.

"Still in the *hammam*. He is talking to my friends. They like him. He is currently in the pool. And he still has that hat on." Sammy laughs so big and loud it drowns out the grizzle of car engines and the rattle of tuk tuk motors. "Deborah Dallow!" Sammy shouts toward the restaurant, "We must go! But you stay and enjoy yourself!", and it's then that Cliff notices Deb is sitting on the veranda with a glass of hot tea, a cigarette in her hand, under the shadow of a waiter who is balancing a colossal wooden rack of flatbreads puffed up like dried-out jelly fish, fresh out of the oven, on his upturned hand. She is trying to ignore him, but he has obviously asked her a question and is awaiting an answer. Rana goes over, says something in Arabic, something which may result in the delivery of a banquet.

"Deb, you will love it here," Rana says. "Best food in downtown Cairo."

"I will be back, Deb," Sammy shouts and he runs to the car. "Wait right there. Howard will join you after his meeting, and then we will be back."

Cliff runs after him.

Lewis after him.

Rana, more gracefully, follows.

"I am not going to lie to you, Robert; the news is not encouraging," Sammy says over his shoulder as the 4x4 speeds through the streets of Cairo.

Oh.

All the running, all the shouting, it definitely felt as if things were looking up.

"So why are we rushing if there's no hope?" says Cliff.

"I did not say there is no hope. We have one last channel for the transfer. But then, I'm afraid we only have one option, really."

"And that is?"

Sammy shifts his large frame so that he can look Rana in the eye.

Rana says, with some disappointment, "We reschedule."

"I thought we couldn't do that?" Cliff says.

"We *can* do it. But we don't want to. It creates much disruption for us. We have discussed this. We will have to show your film as the closing entry," Rana says. "Thursday night."

"I can't do that. I can't be here for that. I made a great many sacrifices to be here for this and I can't stay the whole week."

He looks at Lewis, who is moving his index finger speculatively around and across the screen of his tablet.

Sammy's phone rings.

He speaks only in responses at first, short Arabic phrases, and then in longer sentences, questions; his voice has a metallic weight to it, like the sound of a crane swinging its neck.

He hangs up.

There is a second before he says anything.

"The download failed," he says without turning to face them. "We don't have your movie, Robert. I am sorry."

Cliff feels Rana's gentle touch on his wrist. His head has lowered. He raises it and looks out the window, the conference appearing from behind a hillock of dunes as the 4x4 turns off the highway that feeds out from downtown Cairo to the corporate suburb.

"If only you had brought a copy," Sammy says. "This would have been such a splendid day for you."

Lewis has not looked up from his tablet.

The air is cool, thin, but the lowering sun gives an occasional welcome wave of warmth. Cliff, Rana, and Lewis are sitting outside on the benches of a fast-food stall. Sammy recommended they take some time, give Cliff some air.

Cliff asks the time.

"It is five thirty-eight PM," Lewis responds with pursed lips.

Is that bad? Or is that good?

Sammy said, before leaving them there, that he was going to make a few calls, see if there are any final ideas, but that he is most likely going to ask Zariah to reschedule the screening. Cliff thinks of the words of the critic Mohammed, who seemed generously hopeful that Cliff's film would be shown first. "Last never wins," he had said. "Everyone is tired, full of food and late nights. Most judges snooze through the last film of the competition."

Cliff hadn't been able to gauge whether Sammy was annoyed with him for not taking the meeting with the revolutionaries. Or whether their deal was off. Rana, too, was impossible to gauge; was she still annoyed at Cliff for suggesting his father harboured the plan of a cheat? She sits with them now, as personable as she has been all day. But is she concealing a new distaste for her charge?

There are hundreds of people milling around, but the crowds seem to have thinned. On a small patch of grass children skip and laugh in the spray of a network of sprinklers. Cliff watches them for a moment, smiles at the sight of them, a smile as deep as a ray of sunlight cast across a sheet of glass. He looks at the mothers in a circle sitting a few yards away also watching over them, talking to one another, sharing snack foods from Tupperware, enjoying their children's play. He wants to be home now. He's feeling like the fire of his anxieties has burned its brightest, but still he feels it bristle somewhere inside. It's that moment, shortly after the *fuck it*, when the *does it really matter in the grand scheme of things* takes hold. That's quite a relief, that feeling. His film is dead in the water – it will be rescheduled, but he won't be here, and it won't win anything, not just because he didn't meet the revolutionaries, but also because... you know... it's good, but it's not great. He took too long over it. Tied himself up in knots. He lost the honesty that had been at its conception. And Preston Proudfoot will give Cliff a hard time over not winning, and he won't get another movie financed, not by him, and not by anybody else. But the relief. God, it feels good to be over it. Out of it. Beyond it.

He looks at Rana, enjoying the last sunshine of the day. She probably doesn't see much daylight during the festival.

"You like the sun?" she says to him.

"It's cold at home," Cliff says. "I was scraping ice from the windshield of my car right before we came here. So, yes, this is nice."

"You are worried," Rana says.

He wants to be honest with her and say that he's worried and a little angry, but he looks at the children playing in the sprinklers and feels the sun on his neck.

"I just wish I'd brought a copy of the film," he says.

"I'm sure my father will think of something," Rana says. "It is a very beautiful film, Robert. It has every chance of winning."

Cliff appreciates the sentiment.

Someone is waving at them. A woman, silhouetted by the sun, approaching them.

"I was hoping I'd find you," the woman is saying.

Cliff puts his hand to his brow to try and block out the sinking sun, but still he cannot recognise the figure until she is much closer.

It is Professor Francesca, from the journey from the hotel that morning. She is waving and smiling, full of that energy that puts a spring in her every step.

"I am so glad I found you," she says.

Cliff gets to his feet and they embrace like old friends. Lewis doesn't get up, but he gets a hug too; and Rana exchanges an affectionate bow.

"My schedule – so crazy, I told you, but we have some time open up and it seems to coincide with your screening. There is some healthy controversy on Day One of the documentary competition. An American. He has made a film about a white supremacist hip-hop group. Great, we all thought! Like a Nick Broomfield or Louis Theroux exposé. You know the sort of thing. But then… well… we went into the screening and the lights go down and the first thing that comes up are three quotes, the first from Senator Joseph McCarthy, then one from Leni Riefenstahl, and then one from Tupac. So, for McCarthy we were all thinking this would be ironic, and then there was a red flag with Riefenstahl, but then when the words of Tupac came up… *In one way or another/ America will find a way to eliminate the problem/ One by one…* well, I was shocked, but I was also not the first to stand up and walk out. So, we have disqualified the film from competition. I had a look to see if there was anything to watch now we had relieved ourselves of that dross, and lo and behold, there you were. My friend from the hotel shuttle bus. *The Last January*, at 8pm."

She points to a paper schedule she has held in her hand like a roadmap.

Cliff's face, from a barely concealed grin, drops to something clearly resembling disappointment.

"My friend, what is wrong?" says Francesca, and she takes a seat on the bench next to him.

"We have had some technical issues," Rana says.

"Oh no," says Francesca. "So… no show?" She looks at Lewis. "Good that you have some friends with you, though."

Cliff tries a difficult smile.

"They couldn't get the film over. The file was too big to transfer," Lewis says.

"Oh dear, that is bad luck," says Francesca. "And seems even worse luck considering how easy it is to transfer files like that nowadays."

"Yes," says Cliff.

"It must have been an issue at the other end."

"We think so," says Rana.

"And you tried streaming it from source?" Francesca says.

Silence.

"What do you mean?" says Cliff.

Francesca looks at everyone individually, trying to figure out if she is missing a joke in translation.

Lewis speaks up.

"I suppose she means you could have someone in London upload it to YouTube or something, and then just stream it from that source here directly."

Silence.

"Why has nobody suggested this?" says Cliff.

"There are potential issues with rights," says Rana. "But I think we could get away with it. And it's very unlikely..."

Cliff cuts her off.

"This is it," he says. "This is the chance."

Francesca breaks into an enormous grin, she claps her hands together and says, "Oh this *is* exciting."

The four of them charge back up to Sammy's office.

"If we can get Maggie to upload the film to YouTube then we can stream it direct from there," Cliff says.

Sammy seems unsure.

Rana is already on the phone.

Sammy says it's not ideal.

"But what other option do we have?" says Cliff.

"We are trying to download one last time," Sammy says.

Cliff looks at the download bar.

97 HOURS.

"That is not promising," Cliff says.

"This would have been all avoided if Preston had forwarded you my email," Sammy says.

Everything calms. Everything grows quiet.

There is nothing more to be said for the moment. They all gradually turn to Rana. She has not said anything into the phone for a while. She has not said anything into the phone at all, not at any point.

"Maggie?" Cliff says.

Reluctantly, slowly, Rana shakes her head.

There is no answer.

The download bar clips from 97 HOURS to DOWNLOAD FAILED.

Cliff takes a seat.

"I don't know what to say," Rana says.

"We will reschedule," Sammy says.

"I cannot be here for that," Cliff says.

Sammy looks sorry for it.

Rana looks heartbroken.

Everyone seems to be there now. Zariah looks sad. Bahini looks sad. Lina looks sad.

It's a wake.

Lewis looks at them all one by one, and then his shoulders scrunch as if he's about to say something, and he does.

"Sammy," he says, reaching into his bag, "Maybe now would be a good time for you to look at my script?"

Cliff doesn't even know he's done it until it's done, until the bag is across the room and its contents are strewn across the floor, including the pages of the script, unbound, scattered, and a detritus of stationary, gadgets, discs, pen drives, a couple of graphic novels. Cliff has grabbed it, like a petulant child, and flung it. He also said something filled with expletives, and everyone in the office is now looking at him, the sadness turned to horror, shock, everyone apart from Rana who has averted her eyes and hung up the phone.

Silence.

Stillness.

Cliff rubs the back of his neck.

He can't quite look at Lewis. Cliff knows he's done wrong, that he has embarrassed himself, but he also knows if he looks at Lewis, sees his face, he won't regret what he did, and maybe even will be glad he did it. And that will only make the shame worse.

Oh, the shame.

What is he even doing here? Why did he even make the film? A film that broke him. A film he hates. He can't even remember to bring a copy with him to Cairo.

Cliff walks slowly over to the stuff and gets down on all fours and begins to put it all back into Lewis's bag. Nobody else has moved.

He gathers up the script and puts it to one side in order to arrange the pages when everything else is rehoused in the backpack. It's not so bad down here. He feels he belongs on all fours. He feels this is the least shameful he can be right now. He stops. He lifts himself so he's kneeling.

"What's this?" Cliff says.

"What?" says Lewis.

"This. This disk. It says on it, *The Last January*."

"That must be the copy of your film Uncle Preston gave to me. I must have packed it. Yes, I believe I did now I come to think of it."

Cliff keeps his back to Lewis. He is filling with a heady cocktail of rage and joy and shame and a feeling of inescapable smallness, like he has small thoughts and small ideas and the huge feelings he has connected to this small disk are huge to him and small to everyone else and so he is small and his huge feelings are small; nothing he ever achieves is his own achievement because he is, quite simply, too small.

Cliff stands.

He turns.

Rana and Sammy and Lewis and Francesca and Zariah and Bahini and Lina and the rest of the office are looking at him.

He has the disk in one hand and the bag in the other held there like a vagabond's sack.

"I don't know whether to kick you or hug you," Cliff says in a tone that gives away nothing of his intentions either way.

"You've already thrown my bag across the room which constitutes an act of violence…"

"We have the film," Sammy bellows, cutting Lewis off. Sammy declaims as much in happiness that the fiasco is over as he does that the film is secure and the schedule remains intact. He stomps across the room and takes it from Cliff's hand. "Here," he says to Rana, "keep this *very* safe."

Cliff sees in the corner that journalist from earlier, looking at him, making notes.

Back out in the thoroughfare, Rana brings two beers to the table, a water for her. Lewis has gone to find the bathroom. Dusk is almost over and the warmth has gone with it.

"I want to apologise," Cliff says.

Rana smiles softly.

"We have seen much worse," she says.

"That's no reason for me to not apologise," Cliff says. "I have been shown nothing but kindness and patience and goodwill since I got here."

A moment passes, in which everything seems to be accepted.

"How long are you here?" Rana says.

"Three days."

Cliff rubs his eyes.

"Four days with Lewis," he says, repeating it with a sigh. "I am the worst of the two, I know," he says. "I am under no illusion I come off worse in all this. If Marie was here, she would have given me a right stripping down. Actually, scrap that, she would never have let it get this far."

"It is good you have someone who makes you a better version of yourself," Rana says.

Cliff hasn't really thought of it that way before.

They sit for a while and Lewis returns; his eyes light for a second at the sight of a beer on the table waiting for him. He takes a nip of it.

"Tomorrow morning," Rana says, "I will take you both to the Pyramids. You should see them."

Cliff looks at Lewis.

Lewis hasn't necessarily heard, or listened, to what Rana has just said, but he lifts his beer in an affirmative gesture.

He gets his tablet out.

"Are you nervous about the screening tonight?" Rana says.

Cliff thinks.

"Yes," he says. "And who knows, it could be my last film."

"Every film could be your last," Rana says.

Cliff sips his beer. It tastes good. The best beer always tastes *good*. A solid no bullshit term not open for interpretation. *Good*.

"Can we take a rain check on the Pyramids?" Cliff says to Rana.

"You do not want to see them?" Rana says, surprised.

"I do. I very much do. I was just thinking, let's do it next time. Next time I'm in Cairo. When I'm a better version of myself."

Cliff looks at Lewis again who is drawing with a stylus on the tablet screen. A squid or octopus or something. Music starts up from somewhere beyond them, somewhere in the thickening darkness. And that is where, just about, the story should stop.

Fade to Black.

ACKNOWLEDGEMENTS:

Warmest thanks for the conversations, the support, the thoughts, the inspiration, the facilitating, the work, the feedback, the edits, the encouragement, and the time, to Richard Davies, Carly Holmes, Robert Harries, Kathryn Tann, Sherif Bakr, Hoda H Fadl, Isis Elsherbini, Sara Naguib, Ranya Bakr, Mustafa El-Tayeb, نورالهدى فؤاد, Ahmed Osama, Lloyd Markham, Cathy Costain, Alexandra Buchler, to my family, to Amelia, and to everyone I met in Cairo; you have all had your say in this one way or another.

PARTHIAN Fiction

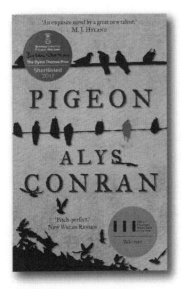

Pigeon

ALYS CONRAN
ISBN 978-1-910901-23-6
£8.99 • Paperback

**Winner of Wales
Book of the Year**

'An exquisite novel by a great
new talent.' – M.J. Hyland

Ironopolis

GLEN JAMES BROWN
ISBN 978-1-912681-09-9
£10.99 • Paperback

**Shortlisted for the Orwell
Award for Political Fiction and
the Portico Prize**

'A triumph' – *The Guardian*

'The most accomplished
working-class novel of the
last few years.' – *Morning Star*

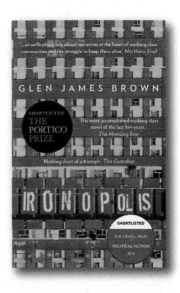

Martha, Jack & Shanco

CARYL LEWIS
TRANSLATED BY GWEN DAVIES
ISBN 978-1-912681-77-8
£9.99 • Paperback

Winner of the Wales Book of the Year
"Harsh, lyrical, devastating... sings with a bitter poetry." – *The Independent*

Love and Other Possibilities

LEWIS DAVIES
ISBN 978-1-906998-08-0
£6.99 • Paperback

Winner of the Rhys Davies Award
"Davies's prose is simple and effortless, the kind of writing that wins competitions."
– *The Independent*

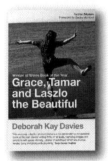

Grace, Tamar and Laszlo the Beautiful

DEBORAH KAY DAVIES
ISBN 978-1-912109-43-2
£8.99 • Paperback

Winner of the Wales Book of the Year
"Davies's writing thrills on all levels."
– Suzy Ceulan Hughes

Hummingbird

TRISTAN HUGHES
ISBN 978-1-91090-90-8
£10 • Hardback
£8.99 • Paperback

Winner of the Stanford Fiction Award
"Superbly accomplished... Hughes's prose is startling and luminous." – *Financial Times*

PARTHIAN Fiction

The Web of Belonging
Out 2021

STEVIE DAVIES
ISBN 978-1-912681-16-7
£8.99 • Paperback

**"A comic novelist of
the highest order."**
– The Times

The Cormorant
Out 2021

STEPHEN GREGORY
ISBN 978-1-912681-69-3
£8.99 • Paperback

**Winner of the
Somerset Maugham Award**
**"A first-class terror story with a
relentless focus that would have made
Edgar Allan Poe proud."**
– New York Times

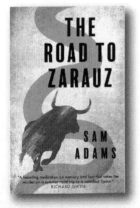

The Road to Zarauz

SAM ADAMS
ISBN 978-1-912681-85-3
£8.99 • Paperback
**"A haunting meditation on memory
and loss that takes the reader on a
summer road trip to a vanished Spain."**
– Richard Gwyn